Unlucky Seven

Dave Zeltserman

Copyright © 2020 Dave Zeltserman

All rights reserved.

This book is a work of fiction. Names, characters, places, and incidents either are the product of the author's imagination or are used fictitiously, and any resemblance to actual events or persons, living or dead, is entirely coincidental.

DEDICATION

To Janet Hutchings.

CONTENTS

Acknowledgments	i
Introduction	1
Brother's Keeper	3
The Last Santa	23
Emma Sue	28
The Caretaker of Lorne Green	38
Some People Deserve to Die	54
A Guilty Conscience	73
Something's Not Right	86

ACKNOWLEDGMENTS

It's Kenneth Wishnia's fault that I wrote Something's Not Right. He needed a story for Jewish Noir, and so I wrote it for him. So blame him!

Janet Hutchings, the esteemed editor at Ellery Queen Mystery Magazine, published three of the stories in this collection, and has always been a source of encouragement, especially at moments when little of it could be found elsewhere, and for that I am eternally grateful.

INTRODUCTION

Oxford Languages defines noir as "a genre of crime film or fiction characterized by cynicism, fatalism, and moral ambiguity."

I love reading noir. I love the dread-induced tension. It's exhilarating following the noir protagonist as he or she desperately struggles against tumbling into the abyss. Horrifying also, which makes sense since there's sometimes a very thin line between noir and horror, although with noir the stakes can be so much higher.

I also love writing noir, but the sad fact is it's a hard sell. While I'm hardly the only noir reader, most crime fiction readers want heroes to root for, and there are no heroes in noir. I was able to publish my first noir novel (and first novel) *Fast Lane* to an Italian publisher before finding a small US press to publish it, and was then able to sell my next four noir novels (*Small Crimes, Pariah, Killer, Outsourced*) to Serpent's Tail while legendary publisher, Pete Ayrton, and equally legendary editor, John Williams, were involved, but things change. Serpent's Tail was bought and stopped publishing American noir, and the remaining market for noir got even tougher. Overlook Press published my sixth noir novel, *A Killer's Essence*, and another novel is set for

German-only publication, and that was it for me. I smartened up, determined not to be like past noir authors who died broke. I switched to writing mysteries, horror, thrillers, and even some fantasy. But there's still a market for noir short stories, and so I keep writing them. This collection is made up of seven of my personal favorites.

BROTHER'S KEEPER

Originally published in the May/June 2019 issue of Ellery Queen Mystery Magazine. A nominee for both the Edgar and Macavity awards for best mystery short story.

The two men who walked into the bar worked for Ned Bishop. Both of them wore dark gray suits with jackets that were a half size too big to better hide their shoulder holsters and provide quicker access to the guns they held. Jack Tomlinson thought the one with the blockier head and cropped gray hair was named Marvin, although he wasn't sure whether it was the man's first or last name. The meaner-looking one with a sharp, angular face and razor-thin lips was nicknamed Nails, and Jack remembered hearing it was because of the thug's penchant for hammering nails into the hands of deadbeats.

Bishop's hired muscle wasted no time in approaching him. The one nicknamed Nails showed a sneer as he appeared to take in the tawdriness of the bar, first glancing at the middle-aged woman sitting alone with a glass of Chardonnay, then at the raggedy couple in a booth before fixing glazed eyes on Jack. Jack, for his part, fought back the urge to slam his fist into the bar. Instead he maintained a friendly countenance as if these men only wanted to order drinks from him. He knew that wasn't why they had come. They were there because of Mitch. The only question was how much money did Mitch owe Bishop this time.

Before Jack could say anything, Marvin put his index finger to his lips and shushed him. In a soft voice that Jack had to strain to hear and sounded almost like a cat purring, Marvin asked about the bar's layout.

"The kitchen's to the right. Down that hallway is a storage room and an office. No basement."

"Any of the doors locked?"

Jack pulled out a keychain, slid two keys off of it, and handed them to Marvin. Marvin handed these to Nails, who headed to the kitchen. He wasn't there long, and then he was walking around the bar and down the hallway that would take him to the other two rooms. Jack smiled pleasantly at Marvin as if nothing out of the ordinary was happening. Several minutes later Nails returned and tossed him the keys. Jack was mildly surprised to see that Bishop's goon had come back emptyhanded and hadn't helped himself to a bottle or two of topflight booze.

Nails told Marvin that there was no one back there. He turned his pale, half-lidded eyes toward Jack. "Not very crowded up front either, is it?" he remarked.

Jack shrugged off the comment. "It's the time of day."

"Nah, I think it's because this place is a dump. Like someone could pick up fleas here if they hung around too long." Nails leered at the woman at the end of the bar. "Or maybe a fleabag."

"The place is clean," Jack said, still maintaining a pleasant demeanor, still playing dumb. "Nothing to worry about, gents. What can I get you two?"

"You gotta admit, Tomlinson, this dive is a big step down from where you used to work," Marvin remarked. "What was the name of that establishment?"

"Stockman's," Jack said, his eyes dulling despite his efforts to show these two nothing.

"That's right," Marvin said. "A classy joint." He showed Jack a pitying smile. "Quite a fall from grace for you, huh?"

"Not really. Just too many bad memories there," Jack said under his breath. When he saw these two walk into the bar, he had promised himself he wasn't going to bail Mitch out this time, but it was a worthless promise, and he had already lost his resolve. It was odd that Nails had searched the bar for Mitch. He'd also caught a certain look in the thug's eyes that told him if he didn't fix this they were going to do worse than just give Mitch a beating. Even if he hadn't seen that, what choice did he have? He had promised his mom on her deathbed that he'd look out for his younger brother. Besides, Mitch was the only family he had left. But dammit, the timing once again couldn't be worse. He was just beginning to dig himself out from the last mess Mitch had left him, but that's the way things always were with Mitch. Two steps forward, three steps back. He breathed in deeply and let the air out in a pained sigh. "How much does my brother owe?"

"That's cute," Nails said.

"You think he's playing dumb?" Marvin asked his partner.

"I don't know," Nails said, his sneer hardening. "It could be genetic. I'm guessing he's the genuine article, like his dumbass brother."

"Seriously, guys, I don't know what's going on. I haven't heard from Mitch in months."

"You're sure about that?" Nails asked.

Jack gave him a confused look. This game playing by them didn't make any sense. He also didn't like the undercurrent of menace that he was picking up from Nails. That this was something more serious than his brother piling up gambling debts.

"Look fellas, as much as I enjoy your sterling company, how about you just tell me what I need to pay to square things for Mitch this time?"

Nails snorted derisively. A thin smile twisted Marvin's

lips as a shadow darkened his eyes. "Seven hundred and twenty," he said.

Now Jack was really confused. Bishop wouldn't send these two thugs to collect a paltry sum like 720 dollars. He'd wait until the vig compounded the amount to at least ten grand before he'd send his muscle to shake Jack down. Maybe this was more serious, like Mitch shooting his mouth off and saying something Bishop took offense at? Could that be what was behind this?

"If you fellas take a seat at the bar, I'll pour you some drinks and get you the money."

Marvin and Nails both sat at the bar. Marvin asked for a Grey Goose vodka martini and Nails told him to leave a shot glass and the bottle of Old Forester. After Jack had them settled, he went to the office and found 645 dollars in the safe. He had enough cash in his wallet to bring the amount up to the required 720. Later, after he dealt with Bishop's thugs, he'd make some calls and try to replenish the money he was borrowing from the bar's safe. If that didn't work, he'd report a robbery at closing time and claim that a couple of punks wearing ski masks forced him at gunpoint to open the safe.

When he got back to the bar, he handed Marvin the 720 dollars. Marvin thumbed through the money and stuck the wad of cash in his pocket.

"Your moron brother owes Bishop seven hundred and twenty thousand dollars," he said.

Jack flinched as if he'd been slapped. "That doesn't make any sense. Why would Bishop extend Mitch that type of credit?"

"These aren't gambling debts." Marvin used his index finger to draw Jack closer, and he lowered his voice so that the woman at the end of the bar and the couple in the booth wouldn't be able to hear him. "Your walking-dead brother ripped Bishop off and left two of his men in the hospital with fractured skulls."

"Mitch wouldn't do something like that."

"The video recording says otherwise."

"Your idiot brother was too dumb to realize there was a surveillance camera," Nails said.

"This has to be a mistake. Someone who looks like Mitch."

Marvin took out his cellphone, fiddled with it, and showed a video of a man with a big goofy grin standing outside a door. It was Mitch. There was no mistaking him. Jack watched as Mitch pulled a ski mask over his head, reached behind him for a big piece of iron, probably a .40 caliber pistol, punched in a code on a keypad, and swung the door open. Marvin turned off the video and stuck the cellphone back in his pocket.

"I got another video of what he did inside the money room, but you don't need to see that."

"Mitch was working as a bagman for Bishop?" Jack asked, incredulous.

"You're joking, right?" Marvin waited for Jack to say something. When he didn't, the hired muscle continued. "We don't know yet how your brother got the location or the security code. He just showed up uninvited, cracked some skulls, and helped himself to Bishop's money."

Nails eyes had taken on the dead, glassy look of a snake's. He said, "You're brother's a dead man. Whether you are also remains to be seen."

Marvin raised a hand to shut up his partner. He said, "You're taking us to your apartment so you can prove to us you don't have Mitch stashed there."

Jack understood fully what was going on. These two goons were trying to size him up and decide whether he had anything to do with the robbery or knew where Mitch was hiding. They must've had orders from Bishop to search the bar and his apartment, but what they really wanted was to get him alone so they could work him over and be convinced that he didn't know anything.

"I'm not going anywhere with you two gents."

Marvin finished what was left in his martini glass, pushed

his bar stool back, and got to his feet. Nails also stood, his arms held loosely at his side, his eyes hooded.

"You don't want a scene here, do you?" Marvin asked in the same soft purr he used earlier.

"I wouldn't be opposed to one."

"If you don't want to take us to your apartment," Nails said, "we can drag you to the office back there and have our private talk there."

"You're betting that I don't have a sawed-off shotgun within reach. Or that you can get to your guns before I blow a hole through one of you."

Jack was bluffing, but he was a good poker player. Better than Mitch, anyway. Nails again showed a hard sneer, but Jack caught a glint of indecision in his eyes. The thug had to know that if there was a shotgun behind the bar, he'd be the one taking its blast.

"It looks like we have a standoff," Marvin said. "Any suggestions?"

"I can promise you you're not finding Mitch without my help."

"We'll make you help us then," Nails said.

"That's not going to happen unless I do so willingly."

"Yeah, well, I think you're bluffing about having a shotgun," Nails offered with disgust.

Marvin ignored his partner. "How much do we have to pay you for your help?" he asked.

"That's not what I want," Jack said. "If I get you back Bishop's money, you let Mitch live."

"That's not an option."

"It's the only way I help. Call your boss. Ask him."

Marvin frowned at the suggestion, but he worked his cellphone out of his pocket and made a call. Jack listened as the hired muscle explained in a hushed tone the situation to his boss. At the conclusion of the call, Marvin's lips pressed into a bewildered smile as if he couldn't quite believe what he had just been told.

"You've got one hour to find your dumbass brother," he

told Jack. "He'll still have to pay a price for what he did. Some broken bones, a few busted teeth, but he won't lose any limbs and we'll leave him alive. If you jerk us around with this to buy him time, you'll pay a price also. This acceptable to you?"

Jack shrugged. "I'd rather visit him in the hospital than the morgue."

Marvin checked his watch. "One hour starting now. And you got to deliver what he stole from Bishop or you'll still be burying what's left of him. Even if it's a dollar short. First, though, you take us to your apartment."

"I don't think so." Jack worked his apartment key off the chain and tossed it to Nails. "Your charming associate can search my place and catch up with us later. If you're only giving me an hour, I'm not wasting a minute of it."

Nails gave Marvin a questioning look. Marvin responded with a nod, and Nails left with the apartment key. Jack waited until the thug was out of sight before using the bar phone to make a call.

"Steve, this is Jack Tomlinson. Yeah, Mitch's brother. You hear from him the last couple of days? That's too bad. You know where Carl Weeks likes to hang out? Donleavy's huh? Okay, thanks. How about Al McCluskey, any idea where I can find him? Hell, that would be great. I'll owe you one. If you get ahold of him, send him to Donleavy's, okay? Tell him I should be there in twenty minutes. That it's a life and death matter. Thanks, man."

Jack got off the phone and told Marvin they needed to get over to Donleavy's in Bushwick.

"Who's Carl Weeks?"

Jack made a shrugging motion mostly with his eyebrows. "A lowlife Mitch has been hanging around with. What I've heard is the two of them have been pulling off short cons at different Brooklyn bars. Small-time stuff. McCluskey is Mitch's sponsor."

"Your brother's in the program?"

"Court ordered. It's not something he takes seriously.

How about giving me back that seven hundred and twenty dollars?"

"I don't think so. Your price for me calling Bishop. And if you don't find your idiot brother, you'll have more serious problems than that money to worry about."

Jack let it go. Marvin was right. That money was the least of his problems right then. He was wearing jeans and a white long-sleeved shirt tucked in at the waist. There was no place he could've been hiding a gun, and Marvin could see that. When he reached for his weather-beaten leather bomber jacket, Marvin snapped his fingers for Jack to hand it over. After Marvin made sure there were no weapons hidden inside any of the pockets, he handed it back. By this time the couple in the booth had cleared out, and Jack informed the woman still nursing a glass of Chardonnay that he was closing the bar early due to a family emergency, but if she came back the next day the first two drinks would be on him.

What Jack had told Marvin about too many bad memories about his former place of work was a lie. The real problem was he had too many regrets to stay there. He had worked at the upscale midtown bar for twelve years, and when the owner decided to retire, he worked out a deal with Jack to buy the place. Even with all of Mitch's screw-ups and Jack always having to bail him out, he'd been able to save up the down payment for the bar. He'd be carrying a hefty loan, but that would be okay—he and Lila had worked out the numbers, and even with the steep monthly bank payments he would still do well. Not enough for them to move to Manhattan, but still enough for him and Lila to have a nice life. Three days before he was set to close on the purchase, Marvin and another of Bishop's goons came to visit him. Mitch had lost twenty grand betting on football, and with the vig compounding for two months, the amount had grown to almost forty grand. They had Mitch stashed away in one of Bishop's properties, and unless Jack made good on his brother's debt, they'd be cutting Mitch up for fish bait. What else could he do? He paid off the debt. Not only did he lose the bar, he also lost Lila.

"You'll always put him ahead of us," she had told Jack. Her anger and frustration had died down, and her face at that moment was heavy only with resignation. "He's an anchor, Jack. Deadweight. He'll drag you down with him. He can't help himself, and you can't help letting him do it. But I'm not going down with you two."

They'd been together six years, and were planning to get married in the spring, but he couldn't blame her for leaving him. He knew she was right, but as she said, he couldn't help himself. It wasn't just that he had promised his mom, but that his bond with his brother was too strong. Jack was four years older than Mitch, and almost from the day Mitch was able to walk he was causing Jack problems. As a six year-old, he'd go up to the biggest kid nearby, tell him that Jack could beat him up, and then kick the kid in the shins. Some fights Jack would win, others he'd have the snot beat out of him. When he would demand to know why Mitch was doing this, his brother would giggle as if it was the funniest thing in the world. When they got older, not much changed. Mitch kept dragging Jack into his messes whether it was him owing money to Bishop, fooling around with the wrong woman, getting caught in one of his schemes, or just plain dumb stuff, like getting Jack sucked into a barroom brawl. Afterwards it would always be the same. Mitch would show his shit-eating grin and apologize in a way that showed he wasn't sorry one bit—that he'd do it all over again if given the chance. If there was ever anyone who exemplified the line '*Who feel that life is but a joke*' from the old Jimi Hendrix song, it was Mitch. But after Jack lost the bar and his fiancée paying off Mitch's debt, his brother seemed genuinely contrite for maybe the first time, and even sounded sincere when he promised that he'd find a way to make it up to him. That was one of the two reasons Jack was convinced Mitch was still in the city—he wouldn't leave without giving Jack some of the money. The other reason was because of Mitch being a screwup. He would assume that he was safe because he had put on a ski mask before raiding Bishop's money room, and instead of going on the run like he should've, he'd hide out for a few days and listen to the grapevine to see who Bishop suspected for the robbery. Bishop must've assumed the same, but still would've had men watching the airports and train stations.

When they got to Donleavy's, which was a hole-in-the-wall bar in what was once a blue-collar neighborhood turning more upscale every day, Marvin checked his watch and informed Jack that he only had forty-one minutes left.

"You can't squeeze blood from a stone," Jack muttered under his breath, not letting Marvin slow him down. There were maybe a dozen people in the bar, and Jack shook his head, letting Marvin know none of them were whom he was looking for. He took an empty bar seat, ordered a beer, and got on his phone. After each call, he grimaced as if he'd been punched in the gut.

"Twenty-eight minutes left," Marvin warned.

"This stress is doing a number on me," Jack moaned. He grabbed his stomach with both hands. "I need to hit the john."

He got off the barstool and moved toward the men's room as if he were a condemned man heading to the gallows. It was an act for Marvin's benefit. He didn't call anyone named Steve earlier. Instead he had called his buddy Dennis Maloney. The name Carl Weeks wouldn't have meant anything to Dennis, neither would Al McCluskey. But Jack had bet that *Captain McCluskey* would. Dennis was a huge *The Godfather* fan who could do a pitch-perfect Brando impersonation and would argue whenever the subject came up that the film was one of the best ever made. He was also someone to call if you needed a piece that couldn't be traced. In *The Godfather*, a gun is planted in the men's room at a restaurant so that Al Pacino's Michael Corleone character could use it to kill McCluskey, and Jack had to hope that Dennis would figure out that he needed a gun planted in the men's room at Donleavy's, which was only a block from where Dennis lived and less than four miles from Jack's apartment in Crown Heights.

Dennis had been sitting at a table when Jack walked in, and he waited until Jack was drinking a beer before walking out of the place without acknowledging him, but Jack caught Dennis's glance toward the men's room. The facilities inside Donleavy's hadn't been updated since the place opened in the sixties, and when Jack examined the near-antique toilet in the lone stall, he found a nine millimeter wrapped in plastic and duct taped inside the tank right above the water line. The magazine was fully loaded, and he said a silent prayer of thanks, chambered a round and secured the gun in his waistband by the small of his back, his leather jacket hiding the pistol from view.

Nails must've made a quick search of Jack's apartment because he had joined Marvin at the bar. He showed Jack a particularly nasty grin and said, "Time's running out for both you and your dumbass brother."

"He's right," Marvin agreed. Another glance at his watch. "You've only got twenty-one minutes left."

Jack finished what was left of his beer, then asked Nails for his apartment key. "You didn't rob me blind, did you?"

"Would it matter if I did? It doesn't look like you'll be going back there."

Jack gave Marvin a questioning look. "I thought if I didn't find Mitch for you, I'd be taking a beating? You're upping the ante on me?"

"I said you'd be paying a price, and that price will be a steep one if you're only wasting our time. Looks to me like that's all you've been doing."

Jack dropped a ten-dollar bill on the bar to cover his beer. "Looks can be deceiving. I've still got a few ideas," he said.

He turned to leave, but Nails moved quickly to step in front of him so he'd be sandwiched between Bishop's two hired thugs, and wouldn't be able to make a run for it in case that was what he had in mind. Nails couldn't have been more wrong regarding Jack's intentions.

Four years ago after Tom Goldsmith, the owner of Stockman's, brought up the subject of retiring and selling Jack the bar, Jack got himself an early morning shift at a warehouse in the Dumbo neighborhood of Brooklyn so he'd be able to save up for the down payment. The way Tom had talked about it, this was at least a few years off, and as long as Jack could save sixty grand by then Tom would help him secure the rest of the financing. Owning a place like Stockman's was his dream and he would've worked three jobs if needed to see that dream come true. Still, he expected only grief and condescension from his brother when Mitch found out that he was now working eighteen hour days; after all, the only "legitimate" jobs Mitch ever took were day labor gigs moving furniture, and that was only so he could scout locations to later rob. Mostly Mitch and his buddies made their money boosting whatever they could off the back of delivery trucks, working their penny ante schemes, and gambling, and in Mitch's case, borrowing heavily from Jack whenever Bishop or another loan shark was out to break his legs. Because of that, it was a surprise when Mitch took an interest in his warehouse job.

"This isn't a gag?" Jack asked.

"No, bro, I'm dead serious about this," Mitch assured him, and for the first time that Jack could remember, his brother appeared serious about something. "It's about time I grow up and get a real job. What do you say, big brother, think you can help me out?"

Jack should've known better.

He brought Mitch in to show him around and introduce him to his supervisor. There were no openings right then, but Jack's supervisor promised to put Mitch's name on the top of the list, and he expected to be able to hire Mitch in no more than a month's time. Eight days later the warehouse burned down. According to the police, the arsonist broke into the warehouse at three in the morning and set the fire using several cans of gasoline. It didn't surprise Jack when he heard whispers in the neighborhood that his brother was selling out of the back of a van the same brand of microwave ovens that the warehouse had had. When he confronted his brother about it, Mitch showed him that same screw-you grin Jack knew so well.

"Not bad, huh?" Mitch boasted, actually proud of himself. "I was able to get fifty-seven microwaves out of the building before the firetrucks showed up. I'm selling them now at a hundred and fifty. All profit. You do the math, bro."

"You destroyed the warehouse for chump change? What the hell were you thinking?"

Mitch made a hurt face as if he couldn't understand why Jack would be upset. "Chump change? Nah, bro, I'm going to clear over seven grand. I had to set the fire to cover my tracks. But what's the big deal? Nobody was hurt and insurance will cover the losses. That company will make out just fine. They'll rebuild and it will be like nothing happened."

It was more luck than anything else that no firemen were injured or killed in the blaze, but Jack was too exasperated to bother explaining that to his brother. No big surprise, Mitch was wrong about nobody losing out. The company might've made out just fine with the insurance, but they decided not to rebuild the warehouse, and instead moved the operations to North Carolina causing over sixty people to lose their jobs thanks to Mitch. The warehouse remained a burnt-out shell and a blight on the area. Jack hadn't thought about it in almost three years, but six months ago he got a call from Mitch asking him to bring over jugs of water, a case of beer, and a weeks' worth of food. "I might need to camp out for a few days or longer until cooler heads prevail," Mitch explained.

If money could've bailed him out, he would've been

asking for that instead. Whatever the mess was, Jack didn't want to hear about it. Resigned to the situation, he asked where Mitch was hiding.

"Remember the warehouse that caught fire? The one that had those microwaves?"

A chain-link fence surrounded the warehouse, but Mitch told Jack how he could get in. Jack loaded supplies into his car, drove over, and found Mitch in the back part of the building. His brother had set up shop there, bringing in a mattress, a beat-up recliner, and a small fridge. Mitch had also rigged up an extension cord from a neighboring building, and when Jack walked in on him, Mitch was fully reclined on the chair, smoking weed, and watching one of the Furious movies on a tablet.

"You like my digs?" Mitch asked, grinning.

"When did you set this up?" Jack asked, amazed.

"Two years ago. When I saw that no one was in a rush to tear this building down, I decided to take advantage of the situation. All the creature comforts of home. I was even able to hack into a Wi-Fi signal from a neighboring building. A perfect hideout, huh, bro?"

Not quite the creature comforts. While faint, the fetid odor Jack detected was enough to tell him that the water and sewer to the building had been turned off, and the toilet Mitch was using had become little more than a latrine. In a week the odor in the place would be unbearable. He also guessed from the way Mitch was scratching himself the mattress and recliner were teeming with creatures that weren't all that comfortable; namely, bedbugs. Mitch seemed particularly annoyed when Jack turned down his brother's offer to smoke weed with him.

"Bro, it's your fault I'm here," Mitch complained, scowling the same as if he were breathing in a stronger version of that fetid odor.

"Why's that?"

"I want to repay what I owe you, at least from last time." Mitch's mouth weakened. "I know what you lost because of last time."

"You don't have to repay me."

"Yeah, well, I'm gonna." For the first time Mitch realized that Jack hadn't brought any supplies with him. "Where's my stuff?"

"In my car."

"I can't go out there, bro. Someone might see me."

"Yeah? You expect me to lug all that stuff back here? Not a chance. Besides, at this hour, the area's a ghost town. No one will see you."

Mitch complained every step of the way, but he accompanied Jack outside, and while Jack sat in his car, his brother made several trips to lug back the supplies. When Mitch was loaded up to make his last trip, he promised Jack he'd be finding a way to pay him back.

"You want to pay me back? Quit this smalltime grifting and get a real job. All of this is getting old."

Mitch flashed him that irrepressible grin. "No can do, bro. But I'll be hitting the big time soon enough. And you'll be getting your money back. With interest."

Jack watched as Mitch worked his way through the cut in the chain-link fence and disappeared into the shadows. He later heard talk that Mitch had tried pulling off a blackmail scheme that soured badly, but as his brother had promised, he worked things out because a week later he was back in the neighborhood boosting what he could off the back of delivery trucks.

This was why Jack brought Bishop's hired muscle to the burnt-out Dumbo warehouse and led them to where the chain-link fence had been cut.

"You're making this so easy us," Nails said as pulled back a ragged piece of the chain-link fence. "Taking us to a deserted warehouse. If your brother's not here, we won't have to wait even a minute to take care of you."

A twisted piece of metal snagged the thug's suit jacket and ripped it. Nails glared back at Jack as if he were blaming him for the accident, and Jack wisely acted as if he hadn't noticed anything.

"My partner's right," Marvin said, huffing as he bent down and pushed his way next through the opening. "If your brother's not here, this will be the end of the road for you, because it sure looks to me like you're going out of your way to waste our time."

"Look, I'm trying my best," Jack insisted.

"Yeah? Give me one good reason why you think he's here?"

"Call it a hunch."

Marvin shook his head as if he were dealing with a slow-witted child. "Your funeral," he said softly under his breath.

Jack led them to one of the entranceways that had been boarded up, and he pulled off loose boards revealing an opening big enough for them to squeeze through if they crouched. Both of Bishop's thugs stiffened when they heard voices from inside the darkened warehouse. The voices were too low to make out, and when they also heard tinny music, they relaxed, realizing that they were hearing a movie being played on a phone or some other electronic device.

"Maybe you do know something," Marvin noted.

They let Jack enter the building first, and they followed him to the back of the warehouse where Mitch was sitting in the recliner smoking weed and watching a movie on a tablet. He started to grin when he noticed Jack, but then froze when he saw Marvin and Nails behind him. For maybe the first time in his life he showed a halfway decent poker face and acted as if he were confused as to why two of Bishop's hired muscle were accompanying his brother.

"Hey, bro, what's going on?" Mitch asked, both eyebrows raised.

"They know you ripped off their boss."

"Bro, I have no idea what you're talking about."

"There was a surveillance camera outside the door of Bishop's money room. Mitch, they have a recording of you."

Mitch blinked several times as if he couldn't quite

understand what Jack was talking about. Then it hit him, and his jaw dropped as he stared at Jack as if he'd been sucker punched.

"You brought them here?" he uttered in disbelief. "My own brother?"

"That's right," Nails said, cracking his knuckles.

"I had no choice," Jack said. "They would've beaten the truth out of me. But I was able to make a deal. If you give them back the money, they'll let you live."

Mitch's eyes deadened for a moment, and then he was back to showing his incorrigible grin. "Wow. That was stupid of me waiting until I got to the door before putting on the mask," he admitted. He pushed himself to his feet, and shook his head as if he couldn't believe his stupidity. "Damn, though, I was so close. But close don't count unless it's horseshoes or hand grenades, huh?"

Marvin said, "The longer you keep us waiting, the worse the beating is going to be."

Mitch's smile turned sickly as he nodded to himself and led the way to a corner of the warehouse. After moving boards and other debris aside, he pulled out a suitcase.

"The money's all there," he said sourly. "I didn't get a chance to spend a dime of it."

Marvin unlatched the suitcase and opened it, showing that it was stuffed with bundles of cash, each bundle fronted by a hundred dollar bill and held in place by a rubber band. Jack caught the way Nails' eyes glazed and recognized it as the look of a stone-cold killer getting ready to act. The thug glided his hand toward his holstered gun. He had no intention of honoring the deal Marvin made, but he moved leisurely thinking he had all the time in the world. Jack, though, moved more purposefully, and Bishop's thug was still pulling the gun from his suit jacket by the time Jack had reached behind him and swung out the nine millimeter pistol his buddy Dennis had earlier left him. He fired two bullets into the side of Nails' skull instantly ending the thug's life.

Marvin looked up, actually surprised. "You don't have to do this," he implored, his voice the same soft purr he had used earlier. "We can work out a deal—"

Jack shot him once in the throat to shut him up. The second bullet went through his eye. Marvin was dead before he toppled to the floor.

Mitch's face froze in a look of stunned amazement, and Jack could almost see the wheels slowly turning in his brother's weed-addled brain as he tried to process what had just happened. Then his brother was grinning from ear to ear.

"I should've known better, bro," he said. "Damn, that was badass of you."

"We need to get out of here now if we're going to escape Bishop. Grab the money."

"Where are we going?"

"Mexico, for starters."

Mitch nodded, his expression intense as he latched up the suitcase and headed toward the exit.

Jack walked behind his brother, and he saw Mitch nearly stumble, his movement awkward and unnatural, and he knew his brother must've somehow realized the problem Jack had been struggling with over the last hour. Jack accepted then that he had only been kidding himself. He never had a choice about what he needed to do. It didn't matter how much money was involved; if Jack brought Mitch with him, his brother would find a way to quickly lose all of it and drag them both down. If Jack split up the money and each went their separate ways, Mitch would inevitably end up in Bishop's hands, and what would be done to him then would be a lot worse than a bullet to the back of the head.

Jack hated that his brother tensed right before he pulled the trigger. He wished it could've been like turning off a light switch. That Mitch would never know what was happening. But he did know. He didn't plead or scream or say anything. He just accepted it. Maybe deep down he knew it was the only thing Jack could do to give himself a chance.

UNLUCKY SEVEN

Jack closed his eyes and said a silent prayer over his brother's dead body. Surprisingly, he didn't feel any guilt or remorse, only relief. He went back to the two dead thugs, searched their pockets, got the car keys for Marvin's car, and both of their phones. He took out the SIM cards and slipped the phones in his jacket pocket. He'd dispose of them later, although none of this was necessary, at least probably not. He couldn't imagine Bishop asking the police for help in locating his two missing thugs.

It would be a long time before Mitch and the two thugs would be found. Probably not until someone decided to finally knock down the warehouse. Not that Jack had anywhere near that time. In an hour or two Bishop would start getting antsy about not hearing from his men. But an hour was all the head start Jack needed. Bishop also had operations in Buffalo, and he would no doubt think that if Jack were on the run he'd be planning to slip over into Canada, and Bishop would have his men looking for him at the wrong border. It would be a longer path to leave the country, but as long as Jack could find his way into Mexico, he'd keep traveling south until he found a small town in Brazil or Argentina where he could buy a bar, maybe find a woman to marry, and live out his days. At least he no longer had a hundred and eighty pounds of dead weight tied to his neck.

On his way out, he took the time to place the loose boards over the opening of what would for now be a mausoleum for Mitch and Bishop's two thugs. After squeezing through the opening in the chain-link fence, he brought the suitcase to Marvin's car and got behind the wheel. He would ditch the car somewhere in Newark, and then find another ride to continue his travels south.

Maybe Bishop would someday find him in whatever sleepy town he ended up in, and he'd have to deal with the consequences of his actions then. Or maybe that would never happen. Jack wasn't worrying about it. If he were to be completely honest about it, even though he took the warehouse job to save up a down payment, deep in his gut he knew Mitch would find a way to screw things up so he wouldn't be able to buy Stockman's, just like his brother would somehow screw things up between himself and Lila. For the first time since his mom died he felt free.

Like he actually had a chance.

THE LAST SANTA

"Ho, ho, ho."

Although Todd Belkins wore a Santa outfit, he shouldn't have been surprised by the urgency the woman used in pulling her wide-eyed little blonde girl away from him. The Santa suit was a mess and he was an even bigger one. The fake beard did little to hide his red-rimmed eyes, rotted yellow teeth, and jaundiced desiccated flesh, and the suit hung on him the same as if it had been wrapped over a scarecrow. He might have had what looked like a pillow stuffed under his shirt, but that did little to create any sort of Saint Nick vibe.

The woman only did what any other mother would do, but Belkins still felt insulted and he had to bite his tongue to keep from commenting about where she could stick her Christmas spirit.

He had been off the junk for a week in preparation for this day and while the jonesing had left him jittery and his thinking scattered and hazy, he still had enough wits about him to know he couldn't risk her or anyone else sending the cops after him. Not with this being maybe his last chance to reconcile with Rebecca and see his daughter, Emma, and not with him having 5,843 dollars of stolen bank loot shoved under his shirt. So he swallowed back the crack he badly wanted to make. This day was too important to let his anger ruin his plans.

The bank robbery hadn't been part of his plans—that was something he had improvised at the last minute because that swindler Desh wanting three hundred dollars for the Santa outfit. Belkins had pointed out that the suit was torn in spots, stained, and smelled like bad cheese. Desh had laughed at that.

"My friend, bad cheese would be a huge improvement over your natural odor. But that doesn't matter. This suit's a money maker. You wear it at the right street corners between now and Christmas, and you'll pull in a thousand easy."

On his good days, Belkins was wobbly enough on his feet as it was and he wasn't about to stand for hours at a time, even if there was a chance of scoring a thousand dollars. But he had a good reason for wanting the suit. Emma always got so excited seeing anyone dressed as Santa, and he knew if he was disguised as Santa he'd have a better than a snowball's chance of getting close to his ex-wife and daughter. The last time he saw either of them, Emma was ten so she'd be fifteen now, and Belkins was certain Rebecca would be taking her for afternoon tea at the Ritz as she had done every Saturday before Christmas Eve since Emma turned five. And so he had to raise three hundred dollars for the damn suit, but *Jesus* it was hard. He was making close to nothing from panhandling and little more than that from his petty thefts.

Things changed when he broke into a car with an NRA bumper sticker and found an automatic with a full clip. His first thought was to rob Desh, but then the cops would be looking for someone dressed like Santa for the crime. It wouldn't help him any, either, if he shot Desh dead since it was well known Desh had the suit. Then he thought of using the gun to rob a bank. He'd never done anything like that, but it took him all of three minutes to walk into the bank, point the gun at the teller, and run out with a bag full of cash. He paid Desh his three hundred dollars and once Rebecca and Emma showed up he planned to give his ex-wife the rest of the money.

He was certain she'd take him back after that. Hell, she'd have to, right? He'll get off the junk for good and things will be better the second time around. Since they'd split, life had spiraled out of control and almost right away he had ended up on the street with a heroin addiction, but before then things hadn't been that bad. He had made good money as a salesman, always busting his ass for his wife and daughter and giving them a better-than-decent home in a well-heeled suburb. Rebecca always had the money to fritter away on her little projects, and he never complained when she did stuff like take Emma on her annual pre-Christmas afternoon tea. He might've joked about her always pissing away his money, but they were only jokes, nothing to take seriously. Given all her getaways and the useless gadgets she bought while he hustled like crazy for her, he had every damn right to those jokes! Jesus, he should've been treated like a saint given all that and her paranoid accusations about what he did when he was away on business trips. It wasn't cheating when you're out of state. Everybody knows that!

An odd sight caught his attention. A fifty-dollar bill fluttering in front of his face. He watched in stunned amazement as a gust of wind took hold and swept the bill away, the fifty dollars swerving down the sidewalk like a drunk bird. It traveled close to thirty yard before a man in a business suit snatched it out of the air. Belkins's eyes locked onto this man's before the man guiltily looked away and, trying to appear nonchalant about it, crossed the street. Only then did Belkins realize that his shirt under the Santa suit had gotten untucked and the fifty-dollars had escaped from him. Panicked, he grabbed a fistful of bills that were about to slip out and frantically tucked the shirt back in, then tightened the black belt to keep the rest of the money in place. He was still clutching a fistful of bill and he shoved these into his right suit pocket, then looked around to see if anyone had noticed him doing this. Probably only the guy who had grabbed the fifty-dollar bill and why would he call the cops? No reason. If anything, he was the thief! As long as Belkins hadn't been leaking other stolen bills he'd be fine. And if he had, he would've noticed it, right? He wasn't that far gone, was he?

He patted his belly or, really, the pile of bills buried under his shirt, and tried to feel if it was as round as it had been earlier. He thought it was. He patted his belly a few more times until he was convinced it was. Only a single incriminating fifty-dollar bill had gotten loose. The cops weren't coming and soon Rebecca and Emma would be arriving. His eyes watered as he thought about seeing Emma again. A tear leaked out and he rubbed it away with the back of his hand. A woman walking past watched him do so.

"This time of year makes me sentimental," he said, his voice choking up.

He looked away from her and steeled his gaze toward the Ritz's entrance. Whatever it took he was going to win Rebecca back. If it meant getting on his knees and begging, he would do it. There was nothing he could do that that would be any more demeaning than these last five years. And really, what reason wouldn't she take him back? Yeah, they had their disagreements, but for the most part they had gotten along even with all of Rebecca's neurotic tendencies. Even with the way she was always smothering their daughter, treating Emma as if she was a fragile piece of porcelain that would shatter if Belkins were too rough with her. Sometimes it was outright insane.

Belkins remembered that time near the end when Rebecca went completely nuts just because he hugged and kissed his daughter. So he had a little fever. Kids get colds, right? You can't bubble wrap them, for Chrissakes. But that still didn't stop Rebecca from going absolutely ballistic.

He squeezed his eyes tight and tried to remember more about that pivotal day. It was early in 2020 before anyone was all that concerned about that virus. At least the president told them they didn't have to be concerned about it. He didn't really think he had the virus and he certainly didn't think Emma would get sick because he hugged her. The little he had read about the virus at that point was that it if you were his age it didn't matter if you got it, and definitely not if you were Emma's age. And Rebecca was annoying the hell out of him, telling him that he needed to move into the garage until they knew whether he was infected. So he just wanted to piss her off, nothing more than that. She made such a mountain over every molehill, and he had gotten damn sick of it.

He remembered what happened next. He became sicker than he'd ever been in his life and within days was coughing up blood barely able to breathe. Soon after that he ended up in the ICU on a respirator. For the next three weeks he was on death's door. But he recovered and was told then that his daughter had died of the same disease…

The realization that Rebecca wasn't coming crashed over him like a tidal wave. More punishing was knowing that Emma was no longer capable of coming…

His legs gave out from under him and he fell onto the sidewalk flat on his ass. A boy no more than ten came running over to him.

He barely had the strength to talk and his voice sounded distant and foreign to his ears as he croaked to the boy, "I ain't Santa. And you don't want to sit on my lap."

The kid didn't rush over to him to sit on his lap, but to grab some of the bills that had busted loose from his shirt. It didn't take long after that for the cops to come.

EMMA SUE

Originally published in On Dangerous Ground (2011). Honorary Mention in Best American Mystery Stories.

Emma Sue's maybe the prettiest gal I've ever seen. I thought so when we were both young and I was courting her, and ten years later I still don't think any differently. She's still a small little thing, no more than eighty-five pounds soaking wet. Her hair's still the same color as fresh cut hay, and with it rolled back in a bun as she usually wears it, it leaves her face so small. As smooth and pink-hued as her skin is most men would have a difficult time guessing that she was any older than the seventeen-year-old gal I talked into marrying me all those years earlier. Most men looking into her clear blue eyes would have no idea about how hard a life she has led since becoming my wife.

Not that there hasn't been some happiness in our lives. I love her enough that I'd cut out my heart for her and I'm pretty sure Emma Sue would do the same for me. But it's been hard for the two of us the last ten years with all the obstacles the good Lord has put in our way as we've tried to run our sheep ranch. The first year a fire burned down our barn and half of our home. I was still rebuilding the barn when an early cold spell hit and wiped out a third of our herd with pneumonia. Emma Sue and I were still struggling to recover from that when three years later a twister struck and tore down both the new barn and most of our fencing. We lost half of our sheep 'cause of that tornado, and six years later were still working ourselves ragged each day to overcome all of that when the final blow was struck. Three months ago a cougar got into our sheep pen and went into a killing frenzy. I should've heard the sheep's bleating, but I was just too bone weary to make sense of their cries. Emma Sue laying next to me slept through it all, dead to the world after spending sixteen hours that day first doing her chores and then tilling the soil and planting hay for the fall. Me, I heard the ruckus, but didn't make sense of it until it was too late. By the time I got my rifle and made it to the pen, the cougar was mauling my last standing sheep after killing all eighty head in the herd. I dropped the cougar with two rifle shots, but it was too late to help me any.

A month later critters even more kill hungry than that cougar took our ranch. The bankers who held the note to our property. I had an offer to work as a ranch hand at the Double Bar, and was able to get Emma Sue a job washing and cooking there, but she would hear none of it.

"If we took those jobs we wouldn't be together," she stated flatly.

That was true. We'd be in different bunk houses. I hated the idea of it since it meant something special having her small body next to mine each night even if we were too exhausted to do much more than feel each other breathing. It gave my life some meaning. But I tried explaining that we didn't have much choice in the matter, and after a few years we'd save enough money to try our luck at ranching again. She told me that nothin' was going to make her sleep apart from me and that we did have another choice. She told me how we were going to make enough money to buy ourselves a farm since she didn't want nothin' anymore to do with sheep. The thing with Emma Sue is she's as tough-minded as she is pretty. As much as I didn't like what she was saying, I knew I had no chance of talking her out of it, and reluctantly went along with her.

We rode out to Tulsa after that. Before we entered Luke Jacobs' Hardware Store, Emma Sue told me we couldn't leave any witnesses.

"The two of us will be caught if we do," she said. "Even if we wear handkerchiefs over our faces, they'll find us. A man and woman robbing the store with me being as small as I am. We have no choice, Bo."

I didn't like it. I didn't see what Luke or his customers ever did to us to deserve what was going to happen to them. Weakly, I suggested we rob the bank that took our ranch instead. She shot me a fierce look. "We do that we'll get caught. Banks can hire posses. No, Bo, this is what we're doing." I knew looking into her eyes there was no use arguing, and besides, I had to admit I didn't see much point in anything if we had to live apart from each other.

As a concession, Emma Sue watched the hardware store from a distance, waiting for when she thought it would be mostly empty. It would be hard for anyone to recognize Emma Sue standing there with the bulky sheepskin coat she was wearing and her cowboy hat pulled low over her eyes so it hid her golden hair. Someone giving her a quick look might even think she was a small man. When Emma Sue signaled, we both strode towards the store from different directions. Emma Sue entered first. When I entered the store I saw that Luke was an old grandfatherly-type with white wisps of hair and a cheery smile. He nodded to me and continued with his pleasantries towards Emma Sue. Outside of Emma Sue and Luke, there was a man about my age studying a shovel. Before I realized it, Emma Sue took two Colt .45s from her coat and trained them on Luke and the customer. I stood mostly in shock at the sight of it.

"What are you waiting for?" she asked, her small knuckles bone-white as she gripped the guns. Luke had frozen up as much as me. The customer with the shovel looked like he was thinking about trying to swing at us. "Oh for lord sake," Emma Sue swore. She shoved one of the pistols in my hand, and I stood dumbly watching as she unsheathed a knife, walked over to Luke and cut his throat as matter-of-factly as if he were a lamb for Easter dinner.

The customer with the shovel decided then he better take action. He swung the shovel back as if he were going to try to knock Emma Sue's head off. I shot him in the belly and he sat down hard on the floor. He looked up at me for a brief moment and then stared at his hands as his guts leaked through them. Emma Sue shot me a disgusted look. She walked over to the dying man and cut his throat also. After that she found the cash drawer and emptied it.

"If you hadn't just stood there you wouldn't have had to fire any guns and brought us attention," she scolded me in a breathless whisper. "Now get moving!"

As we agreed earlier, I left the store first. My gunshot hadn't attracted any interested parties. I got on my horse and waited until Emma Sue left. I watched as she rode off, flashing me just the barest of looks. A half hour later we met up, all the while my heart was racing with worry over Emma Sue.

"Why'd you freeze back there, Bo?" she asked me.

"Those two back there didn't deserve killing."

"Life is full of suffering," she said. "I'm just sick of it being us all the time. Bo, we're just doing what we have to. It would kill me having to live apart from you, and I'd think it would kill you having to do the same. I ain't going to let that happen to you."

I nodded 'cause I knew she was right. "How much was in that cash drawer?" I asked.

"Eight hundred dollars."

Eight hundred dollars was more than we had thought going in, but I still couldn't help being disappointed. We figured we needed three thousand dollars to start over, and this meant we'd have a lot more killing to do before we were done.

"It's a good start," she said. "In a week we'll ride out to Chandler."

"You ain't doing no more killing," I said.

She gave me a hard look then, her blue eyes piercing deep into mine. "As long as you have the strength to do what has to be done," she said at last.

"I'll have the strength," I insisted.

We spent the next four hours riding to Muskogee. We didn't talk much during the ride, and I tried hard not to think of Emma Sue cutting those two men's throats. We lived it up in a motel the next week, but I couldn't get myself to touch Emma Sue. She didn't say anything, being too proud a woman, but I knew it hurt her. And I knew it wasn't right on my part. She did what she did for me. But news had spread about the slaughter at Luke's, and I just couldn't quite look at Emma Sue the same way, at least not until we rode off to Chandler. By then I had accepted what had happened, and as we exchanged glances I could see that she knew there were no longer any problems between us. We stopped at the town of Sapulpa, checked into a fancy hotel they had there and made up for the past week. The next morning we rode straight to Chandler. When Emma gave the signal, I strode straight into the Chandler General Store, and without breaking stride got behind the storekeeper and cut his jugular. There was a woman in the store and she started screaming. Emma Sue had her gun pointed at her, and I could see her knuckles growing bone white but I'd be damned if I let her do any more killing. As savage as that cougar must've been with our herd, I was on that woman damn near cutting her head off. When I looked up Emma Sue was emptying the cash drawer. Before either of us could move a boy entered the store. He was skinny, no more than ten, and had a big grin on his face until he spotted the carnage and made sense of it. The grin disappeared then and his skin paled to the color of milk. I could see the alarm in Emma Sue's eyes as she pointed one of her colt .45s at the

UNLUCKY SEVEN

boy. I was up and tackling the boy before he could run. I had a hand over his mouth as I swung him to the floor.

"We can't leave any witnesses," Emma Sue was saying. "That boy can get us both hung."

I nodded, trying not to look at the fear flooding in the boy's saucer-wide eyes. I tried just as hard not to hear the pounding of his heart.

I could feel Emma Sue staring hard at me. "You don't have it in you to handle this," she said.

"I do too," I forced out. "Besides, you ain't doing any more killing."

There was a long moment where Emma Sue just stood and stared at me. "I'll wait until you do it," she finally said.

"You ain't seeing no more killing either," I said. "I'll do it. Just leave first."

She took my knife from me and wiped the blade clean. "I want to see blood on that blade," she said. "If there ain't any, I'm coming back and doing what you can't."

"I'll do it," I promised. I waited until the door closed behind her, then I dragged the boy over to a bundle of rope, cut off some pieces and tied him up.

"I don't want to kill you, boy," I whispered to him. "You understand?"

He nodded, his eyes growing even wider with terror.

"You ain't going to tell no one what you saw here, right?"

He nodded.

"You don't know what we look like. You were hit from behind. That's what happened, right?"

He nodded again. I took my hand away from his mouth. "You promise on your mother's grave?" He tried to answer me but a sob choked him off. The tears welling in his eyes started to leak down his face. "I need to hear it," I said. So low that I could barely hear him, he swore on his mother's grave. I rolled my handkerchief up and pushed it into his mouth. "I'm sorry I have to leave you like this," I told him. "But I got no choice. Now close your eyes."

After he closed his eyes I got up and wiped the blade across the open wound on the storekeeper's throat. I didn't want the boy to have to see that.

When I left the store and rode away from Main Street, Emma Sue was waiting. She made me show her the bloody knife blade. "We just can't leave any witnesses, Bo. If we do they'll catch us."

I didn't say anything. I just watched for a moment as she rode off. It was an hour later when we caught up together where we had planned.

"Bo, you did only what you had to. You did it for us."

I gave Emma Sue a hard look, hoping she couldn't see the truth in my eyes. "How much did you get?"

"Eleven hundred."

She reached over and squeezed my hand. "Maybe just one more time, Bo, and we'll have enough."

I put my free hand on top of hers, but I couldn't look at her. I couldn't let her see how I had betrayed her. How I had betrayed the two of us. That boy was going to talk. I knew the woman I killed in the store was his ma. I could see the resemblance in their eyes and the shape of their faces. I was kidding myself thinking that I didn't have to kill him, that he wouldn't give a full description of both of us. Now they'll be looking for a man with a small, slender woman. They'll know what both our faces look like. Our only chance now was to ride far enough away. Or hope that boy's description wasn't good enough.

Emma Sue and I had decided to go next to Abilene, which is a hard two days ride. Our plan was to wait out all the news of the slaughters and then ride up to South Dakota to finish what we needed to, but I decided that I was going to talk her into riding east instead, that we had enough money to buy a small store in Boston or some other city where no one would ever hear of the goings on in Tulsa or Chandler. The first night we camped out under the stars. It was so quiet I could barely stand it. Emma Sue noticed my unease and sidled up to me, resting her head against my chest. Her wheat colored hair had been taken out of its bun, and now flowed halfway down her slender back.

"I know it was hard what you had to do," she said. "But you did it for us, Bo."

I stroked her hair but didn't say anything. All I felt I could do was stare at the vastness above me.

It was two days later when we arrived in Abilene and checked into the Victorian-style hotel they had downtown. Emma Sue was delighted when she saw the room. "Ever think we'd be in such a room?" she asked. Chambermaids filled up a bathtub that was right there in the room and I watched as Emma Sue took a bath, the water sudsing up from the fragrant salts that had been added to it. I don't think I ever saw Emma Sue happier, and while it made me smile, I couldn't stop worrying.

It was two days later when rumors started to spread about the slaughters that occurred in both Tulsa and Chandler. I wanted Emma Sue and me to stay hidden in our hotel room, but she just laughed off the idea.

"There's nothing to fret about, Bo. No one saw us. Now I hear the saloon has the best steaks in Kansas and that's where we're eating!"

I should've told her about the boy, but I couldn't build up the courage to do that. As we were walking back from dinner, we passed two men who turned back to stare at us. I tried not to look, but I could see them whispering and pointing at us. Emma Sue noticed it to, and I could see the consternation ruining her brow.

"What do you suppose they're whispering about?" she asked me, suspicion flashing in her all-too blue eyes.

I didn't answer her. I just grabbed her by the elbow and hurried her along.

"You didn't kill that boy, did you?" she accused in a harsh whisper.

"Not now," I said.

When we got back to the hotel room, Emma Sue was ashen. "You didn't do it. You left that boy alive to identify us."

"That boy was too scared. He didn't know what he was seeing."

"Yes he did." Emma Sue sat on the bed. She looked so small as she clasped her hands together and tried hard not to cry. "I don't want to lose you, Bo. But I'm going to."

"You won't," I told her. "We can ride out now. If we head East, we can disappear someplace like Boston or New York."

"It's too late," she said. "They know we're here. We won't be able to outrun them."

I heard a commotion from outside. Emma Sue heard it too. I pushed the curtains aside and saw a mob outside the hotel. The two men who had been whispering and pointing at us were talking to the hotel's desk clerk, and were now running into the hotel. Emma Sue had joined my side and watched it also.

"Don't let them hang me," she pleaded. She grabbed me hard and buried her face in my chest. I could feel my shirt growing wet. "Please, Bo, not that."

I tried holding her, but she pushed away from me. "Please, Bo, if you love me as much as I love you, don't let that happen. I can't bear the thought of that, having them all stare at me dangling from a rope."

Then she lay down on the bed and waited.

I didn't want to move, but when I heard them banging on my door, I had no choice. I loved Emma Sue more than life. I couldn't let that happen to her. I couldn't stand the thought of them pawing and grabbing at her, or worse, leering at my Emma Sue as they strung her up. I did what she wanted me to do. I took one of the fine goose feathered pillows and held it over her face until she was gone. My heart was still beating, but I was as dead as she was. All that was left was to open the door and let the mob finish the chore.

When I met them standing outside the door I held out my hands to make it easy for them. One of the two men who had been whispering and staring at me and Emma Sue grabbed my right hand and started pumping it.

"Bo Wilson of Pawhuska, I knew I recognized you."

Slowly, I recognized him also. He was Tom Laraby. I recognized the other man too. Albie Henricks. I hadn't seen them since I started sheep ranching, but they both grew up where Emma Sue and I did.

Tom Laraby stuck his red face into the room and spotted Emma Sue laying on the bed. "I'm sorry," he said in a hushed whisper. "I see your wife is asleep. Still as pretty as ever. I didn't mean to disturb you two but we're forming a posse to go after some lowdown thieves who robbed the First Abilene Bank earlier."

Albie Henricks chimed in that it was the same men who did the massacres at Luke Jacobs' and the General Store in Chandler.

"That's right," Tom Laraby said. "They left a boy alive at the store in Chandler. According to him it was two men, a small one and a large one, just like the two who robbed the First Abilene. Anyway, bank's offering fifty dollars a head and when I recognized you on the street, I thought you might want to join us. Always on the lookout to help a fellow Pawhuska."

I thought how Emma Sue was at the store in Chandler. With her heavy sheepskin coat and her hat pulled down low, as fearful as the boy was he never realized she was a woman. We would've been safe. I nodded to Tom Laraby, then went back into the room and grabbed my gun and coat. When I came back to join the mob, Tom Laraby gave me an odd look. "Ain't you going to wake your wife to tell her you're going?" he asked.

I shook my head. "Better just to let her sleep," I said. If I was lucky I'd be killed on the ride. Otherwise they could hang me later when I came back. Either way it didn't much matter.

THE CARETAKER OF LORNE GREEN

Originally published in the August 2016 issue of Ellery Queen Mystery Magazine This story was written as a response to a friend joking about the title of my similarly titled horror novel.

I'm a half hour late getting the old guy out of bed and that must be why he's in such a sour mood. After I wheel him into the bathroom, I put him in a bear hug so I can lift him from his wheelchair and deposit him into the tub, and he sits sulking, his thick lips curved down into a steep frown. He doesn't utter a peep the whole time I'm scrubbing his back with a brush, nor later after I get him back in his chair and shave him and clip his nose and ear hairs. I don't much feel like doing any of that this morning, but if I don't he'll be crying about it all day.

I'm hoping he stays pouting like this. I can use a day without him yakking. But no such luck. After I get him dressed and sitting at the kitchen table for his cereal and morning coffee, his mood perks up and he gets talkative.

He exaggerates a wink at me. "You want to guess how much action I used to get?" he asks.

"I'm guessing a lot."

"Damn straight! You want to know why?"

UNLUCKY SEVEN

I play my part and say like he's expecting me to, "It's got to be 'cause of how much you look like that actor, Lorne Greene."

That cracks him up and he starts laughing, these wheezing, cackling noises coming out of him, his face reddening. When I was a kid I used to watch *Bonanza* reruns, and if I squint hard enough I can see the resemblance in his round, wrinkled face, even though on first appearance it looks more like a deflated basketball with a couple of caterpillars glued on than the face of any famous actor. But then again, the old guy's got to be at least eighty, so it's not fair of me to judge him the way he is now with his caved in chest and bald head and wrinkly old face covered with moles and growths. When he was younger, he might very well have looked like Ben Cartwright from the Ponderosa. I imagine how he might've been with broad shoulders, a younger, more robust body, and his own teeth instead of the cheap dentures stuck in his mouth, and I can almost see it.

"That's right," he says when he can, although he's still laughing so hard the words come out in these gasping wheezes. "Back then I had a deep baritone voice, just like he did. When I told the girlies I was Lorne Greene, a lot of them believed me right away. The ones who thought I was only kidding around changed their minds after I showed them my driver's license."

His frog-like, raspy voice is grating on me and starts bringing about a headache. We've already had this same conversation at least a dozen times, maybe more. But like any good straight man, I feed him the line he's expecting. "If they looked closely enough, they would've seen your last name's spelled differently."

"You bet it is," he says, his wheezing laugh dying down, his expression growing peevish. "I don't got that extra 'e' at the end. The judge wouldn't allow the same spelling. He thought I was trying to pull a fast one changing my name to Lorne Greene, and tried telling me I had a perfectly fine name with Arnie Crenshaw and that I should just keep it as it is. What the hell did he know? Why would I keep a name like that when I could get all the action I could handle by changing it? I told him, your honor, I'm over twenty years younger than that actor. How could anyone in their right mind mistake me, a thirty-two year-old guy, for some actor in his late fifties? But I couldn't get him to budge."

"He was being unreasonable."

His lips pucker in and out as if he's tasting something bitter. "Damn straight he was," the old man spits out. His eyes dull as if he's lost in a memory, then he shrugs and continues, "We dickered back and forth until he finally agreed to let me change it to *Lorne Green*, without the 'e'. The joke was on him. Lorne Greene was the actor's stage name. His real name was Lyon Green. Whenever a lady noticed the difference in the spelling on my license, I'd tell her how *Greene* was my stage name, and they almost always bought it." He slaps his knee and starts cracking himself up again and says, "I remember these sisters in particular when I was traveling through Kansas City. Three of them—"

I try to tune him out and not listen to how he bagged those three Kansas City sisters on a rainy afternoon some forty years ago. I've heard the story several times already. I must've heard all of his stories by now, and his voice is now like nails on a chalkboard. I can barely stand it. As he blathers on I wait for him to take more sips of the instant coffee I made for him. Earlier I had ground up half a sleeping pill and stirred the powder into the drink. He's already had enough of the doped coffee that he's slurring his words and his eyelids are drooping. Another few minutes and he'll nod off. That should give me a couple of hours of quiet, and time to search more of the house. If I didn't have to worry about a relative or social worker or someone else dropping by, I'd gag him and tie him up until I find where he has his money hid.

Thirty-eight days ago I was working as a bag man for Big Joe Lombard. He had me that day laying bets at the track to hike up odds for the horse he had fixed to win the fifth. I'd decided the night before if the odds got rich enough I'd use that race as my ticket out of town, and when they hit forty to one, that was it. I'd held back two grand of what I was supposed to be spreading around, and I used that to sneak a bet on the winner. I knew Big Joe would want me dead for that, but that would be his tough luck. The eighty grand payoff was going to send me far enough away so I'd never again have to worry about his ugly kisser, as well as leave me flush enough to start something on my own.

All afternoon at the track and I didn't once spot any of Big Joe's muscle so I thought I was home free, but I guess that's just what guys like me always think. After the fifth race finishes, standing sentry duty by the betting windows was Vinnie Paz, maybe the meanest and most vicious of Big Joe's crew; a leg breaker who enjoyed his work way too much. I might've had a chance of convincing Big Joe that I wasn't the one who double-crossed him if I had turned around and disappeared back into the crowd, but I froze trying to think of a way to bribe Paz so he'd let me collect my winnings. This was only for a second, maybe two, and I should've known that there was no way of me doing that—that Paz enjoyed hurting people more than he enjoyed money so he wasn't about to risk his dream job for any bribe. The instant he spotted me and I saw the way his eyes transformed into what you might see on a rattlesnake, I understood that. The only thing that saved me from being bumped off by Paz then was an old lady with a walker stepping in front of him the split second he was gearing up to run after me, and in his haste he tripped over her. That was what gave me the head start I needed, and I raced out of there to my car like I had a rabid dog hot on my heels, which in a way I did, all the while my pulse pounding like a jackhammer in my temples. I couldn't risk looking behind me. If I did it would've slowed me down enough for Paz to get me. As soon as I got behind the wheel, I shot out of there burning rubber.

The first few miles I drove recklessly to lose Paz or

anyone else who might've been following me. Doing stuff like flooring it through red lights and taking hard turns at the last possible moment. When I was sure it was safe, I pulled into a strip mall so I'd have a chance to think. I had to get out of town, but my credit cards were maxed out, and I didn't even have enough cash to fill up the tank. It would be too risky hitting up any so-called friends for loans—Big Joe probably already had the word out and I'd be ratted out in a second. All I could come up with was selling my car—which was little more than a rusted out piece of junk—and using the cash for a bus ticket. I wouldn't get more than two hundred for it, but at least it would get me far enough away from Big Joe so I'd be able to breathe easy. So of course after wracking my brains and settling on that plan, I couldn't get the car started up again, the engine making a sick whirring noise.

There was no use sitting there feeling sorry for myself—I couldn't afford to do that, not with Big Joe hunting for my scalp—so I went across the street to a gas station and had them tow over my car. Once they got it fixed, I was going to rob the place. I didn't see as if I had any choice since I wouldn't have the money to pay them. After a half hour of sitting around, the mechanic came over to me, a funny look on his face.

"Someone shot a bullet through your gas tank," he said.

I might've blinked when he told me that, but I can't say for sure. Paz must've used a silencer. I didn't even know he had gotten close enough to fire a shot at me. But I played innocent and said, "No kidding? So how much to fix it?"

He scratched behind an ear. "I'll have to call around and see what a replacement gas tank goes for, but a rough guess, thirteen hundred." He paused, and somewhat dubiously asked, "You want it fixed?"

"The car's not worth anywhere near that."

"Nope, it isn't."

"How about I sell it to you for parts and scrap metal? A hundred?"

His eyes got shifty as he knew he had me over a barrel since it would cost more than a hundred to tow the car somewhere else to sell it. "I can give you fifty," he said.

I took the fifty. What else was I going to do? Since I expected to go on the run after the fifth race, I had the title with me, and I signed it over. I also had a packed suitcase in the trunk. I no longer thought of robbing the place. It would've been too risky with my car out of commission. Let's say I boosted one of the other cars there, the odds were it would have a tracking device hidden somewhere in it and I'd be caught by the cops within an hour. Besides, while I was waiting, I thumbed through a newspaper that had been left behind, and spotted an ad in tiny print for a caretaker job not too far away. That got me thinking it could be a good place to hide out until things cooled off with Big Joe, and when the time was right, a hell of an easy place to rob.

If I'd asked, I'm sure I could've gotten a ride, but I wasn't going to let anyone at that gas station know where I was going. If Paz realized he hit my gas tank, he'd be searching all the nearby garages and gas stations for my car, and he'd soon know whatever the guys in the gas station knew. So I set off on foot with suitcase in hand, and I probably sweated off ten pounds as I walked the two miles to the address given in the newspaper, and I also jumped a bit in my skin at every little noise. I damn near had a heart attack when a car pulled up next to me, but it was just some guy asking directions.

I got to the address in one piece, which was for a big Victorian showing some signs of disrepair. Not that the house was falling apart, but paint was peeling, a couple of shutters hung loose, windows needed to be cleaned, the yard nothing more than dead grass and dirt. I walked up the driveway, which was broken up and had weeds higher than my knees growing from the cracks. From there I cut over to the front door and tried ringing the bell, which didn't work, so I used a badly tarnished brass knocker instead.

When the door opened, it was by a large black woman of maybe fifty who first scowled at the suitcase I was holding and then set the scowl on me.

"What you here for?" she demanded in a heavy Haitian accent.

"The caretaker position advertised in the paper. It's not filled, is it?"

She gave me a look that could only be interpreted as 'not by me, thank Jesus', which was a lucky break for her. No matter what, I had decided I would be using that house as a hideout, even if it meant stacking bodies in the basement.

"The job's still open," she said. "I'm here temporary." Another *thank Jesus* type look flashed on her face. "You got any experience?"

"Would I've brought my suitcase if I didn't?"

She didn't question me further on that, and instead turned and told me she'd have me meet the old man, mumbling a word in front of 'old' that sounded like it could've been *crazy*, but I wasn't sure.

The hallway we walked down was poorly lit, and the air inside smelled stale. Not dirty, but still not too pleasant. The furniture was all old and dull, but looked like it must've cost some dough when it was first bought. She led me into the kitchen where the old man was eating beef stew that had been heated up from a can. I would learn later that he had a basement stocked with several years supply of canned food and boxes of cereal and crackers. Not one thing fresh in the house. Even the milk he used for his cereal and coffee came from cans of evaporated milk, which was a surprise to me anyone still sold that stuff in the States.

The old man stared at me, his expression turning sour. "What he's here for?" he asked suspiciously.

"The caretaker position you advertised for," the Haitian woman said.

"You fool. He's here to rob me. I bet that suitcase is empty!"

As I said, I was going to do things the hard way if

needed, but I preferred not to have to, so I put the suitcase on the table and opened it to show him that it was filled with clothes.

The old man sniffed in an injured sort of way as he peered into the suitcase, his manner growing increasingly sullen. "I still don't want him," he stated.

The Haitian woman ignored him and told me what my duties would be outside of the obvious ones. "He thinks he's a ladies' man," she said with disdain. "He wants to be groomed every day like he's got a hot date, so you need to shave him, clip his nose and ear hairs, and scrub him pink in the tub. Every day. You can work out your salary requirements with him."

"Are you deaf?" the old man croaked out angrily. "I said I don't want him!"

She faced him, hands on hips, a hotness in her eyes. "I told you I was here only temporary until you find someone fulltime. I've had enough of you! And you better mail me what you owe me!"

She turned then and stormed out of the room. She couldn't have been sleeping in the house 'cause she didn't bother collecting any clothes or belongings; instead seconds later the house rattled from her slamming the front door.

"Who needs her," the old man muttered under his breath, then he eyed me cautiously. "I got a daughter who lives nearby," he said. "She checks up on me all the time. You try something and she'll know it."

"I'm just here to do the job you advertised for."

He made a face as if he didn't believe me, but he still went about negotiating a price with me. He quickly got cagey and insisted on a two-month trial where if things didn't work out he wouldn't owe me a cent. I didn't care. I knew he was lying about having a daughter checking up on him. It didn't matter. Even if there was no daughter in the picture, he still might have someone who came by occasionally to check on him—maybe someone from social services or a local elder affairs office. Because of that I would play along and do my job as caretaker. I had to since I was planning to be there for a month, if not longer—and not just so I could hide out from Big Joe. It was so I could find where he had his money stashed. I knew he had a lot of it stashed somewhere. I knew it because I knew the guy's a swindler. I can always recognize a fellow member of the guild.

I was proven right early on when I found two grand hidden in a hollowed out bible. That's an old swindler's trick—keeping easy-to-grab money hidden about in case you need to take a quick powder. Without much sweat I found another six grand scattered around in false bottoms of drawers and places like that. I left all of the money where I found it—I'll be grabbing it when the time's right, but I knew he's got a significant stash hidden someplace where it will take a serious effort to get to it, and that's the money I want.

Four days ago I learned I underestimated the old man. That was when I found newspaper clippings from fifty-five years ago. These were hidden in the crawlspace of the attic and were about a kid from a rich family who was snatched, which all but told me the man who changed his name to Lorne Green was more than simply a swindler. Instead he started off as a kidnapper. None of the clippings mentioned how much money was paid out, or whether the kid was ever returned. But I knew Green must've gotten a bundle from that job. He would've been around twenty-five then, and I doubted any of the ransom still remained, but I knew he must've done other jobs. Somewhere in this house was a pot of gold waiting for me to find it.

I pull up a floorboard in the back of the old man's closet, and that's where I find the jewelry. There's not just jewelry. Under each piece—and there's got to be at least thirty of them—there's a photo of a woman. In some cases they're Polaroids, in other cases they're wallet shots. Some of them show the woman posing with a big smile, in others the subject doesn't look too happy. Three of the Polaroid shots, the girls alike enough where they must be sisters, and it makes me think of his Kansas City story.

This is the old man's trophy case—he must've stolen items from each of these women as a keepsake. I'm sure he must've robbed them also. As I look over the jewelry there's one piece that's trying hard to get my attention. A diamond ring that keeps winking at me.

I pick it up for closer inspection, then take it to the window so I can see it under sunlight. I'm no expert, but I'm no amateur either, and I'm guessing the ring's around three carats, and it looks flawless to me. This could be worth some serious dough. Maybe twenty grand, maybe a lot more. I start feeling antsy thinking there's a chance it might be glass. I pocket it and start down the stairs. When I hit the first floor, I can hear the old man snoring away in the kitchen. I continue on down to the basement where there's a tool chest. I wrap the diamond ring in a rag, and then whack it as hard as I can with a hammer. It's not glass. There's not a scratch on it. It might be cubic zirconia, but I don't think so. I'm pretty sure it's the genuine article. My palms start itching. I decide I've been hiding out long enough. Hard to believe Big Joe would still be scouring the city for me, so it's time for me to collect my payday and scram. The eight grand I found, this diamond, the other jewelry—it will add up to a nice piece of change, but I want much more. I'm either going to make the old man tell me where he's got his stash hidden, or I'll start pulling down walls until I find it.

I jostle the old man awake. At first he's still groggy from being drugged, his eyes glassy as they crack open. But when he spots the diamond ring and the eight grand sitting on the table out of arm's reach, he straightens up, his eyes clearing quickly.

"I knew you were only a cheap thief," he croaks out as he glares at me with contempt.

I don't bother arguing with him. What's the point?

Besides, he's mostly right. I don't kid myself otherwise, but the cheap part will be changing once I get my hands on his hidden fortune.

"This is either going to go easy for you or hard," I say. "The easy way is you tell me where you got your money hidden, then I lock you up in the food pantry and call the cops after I get out of the country. The hard way is I start beating you 'til you either talk or you drop dead. And if you drop dead before you talk, I'll tear the walls down and dig up the floors if I have to to find where you have it hidden."

He lowers his eyes from mine and he sniffs in the direction of the eight grand sitting on the table.

"You already found it," he says, his tone injured.

"That's only your emergency fund. I want what you got from a lifetime of kidnapping eleven year-old boys, and cheating and robbing women."

He looks toward some faraway place, his face a blank mask. "Go to hell," he mutters in a raspy croak.

I sigh loudly enough so he can hear how put upon I am that he's going to make me beat him. I first wheel him away from the table, then I reach down so I can pull him from his chair and dump him onto the floor, but he moves with surprising speed, his right fist a whirl as he clocks me on the jaw. The blow staggers me back a couple of steps, and I watch with stunned surprise as he bolts from the chair and races out of the room.

I snap out of it quick enough. The punch leaves my jaw throbbing, but he didn't break anything, and I find myself grinning over how he faked me out for weeks making me think he's an invalid. I hear him rummaging about in the room set up as a den, and I move quickly to chase after him, thinking he's going to be on the phone calling the cops. But he's not worrying about the phone. Instead he's thrown books off a built-in bookcase and slid a panel off to a cache of some sort. When I see what he's pulled out of the cache, I charge him, the adrenaline pumping hard in me, and I hit him with a tackle knocking him to the floor. The two of us struggle over the gun that he's taken from the wall. Both of us are clawing at each over as we roll around, and it's a tougher fight than I would've thought. Even at eighty he's a powerful man, and for a moment I think I'm going to die, but I get the gun barrel tilted enough so when the trigger's pulled the bullet strikes him under his chin. His body sags and I know he's dead even before I see the mess that was made when the bullet exited his skull.

I'm shaky as I get to my feet. I never killed anyone before. Thirty-eight days ago I was just a bag man and a low-level chiseler, but because I had to outsmart myself over a fixed race I'm now something very different.

I don't know how loud the shot was. To me it sounded like a bomb exploding, but maybe that was just the way it was to me. Maybe the old man's body muffled the sound. Maybe none of the neighbors heard it. I look down and see my shirt's splattered with blood, and I understand immediately why my face feels sticky. No matter what, I have to clean myself off and change into clean clothes. If the cops come, there's nothing I can do about it. But I know I don't have time anymore to tear apart the house. I take a look in the hole in the wall Green had exposed. There's more newspaper clippings, a passport, nothing else.

While I'm washing the blood off me and then changing into new clothes, I have an idea what I need to do. No more than five minutes and I'm back downstairs bringing my suitcase with me filled with the rest of my clothes, including the ones made bloody by the shooting. I leave the suitcase in the kitchen, add to my wallet a thousand from the eight grand, and put the rest of the money in a bag holding Green's stolen jewelry. I put the diamond ring in my pocket. After I turn the gas on in the oven, I leave the kitchen.

After I move to the den, I wipe off any prints from the gun, take hold of Green's corpse by his ankles and drag him back to the kitchen. I use a trash can to start a fire and feed it with enough old newspaper to keep it burning. I think about those newspaper clippings that Green had kept with the gun, and I almost go back for them since I'm curious what they're about, but instead I leave the house through the backdoor, mostly because I don't know how much time I've got with the gas from the oven filling up the kitchen.

It turns out I didn't have much at all. I had cut across the backyard and was stepping onto the street running behind Green's when the explosion happens. I turn around to see the flames, and then I'm running to get as far away from there as I can.

An hour later I'm at the bus depot with a ticket in hand that will take me to Cleveland. I have no interest in going there but it's the first bus out of town and it's boarding in fifteen minutes. The minutes ticking off are torture. I'm keeping my face hidden behind a newspaper, but I can't stop worrying about Big Joe's being tipped off that I'm here. I know I'm just being paranoid—that it's only nerves—but I can't shake the feeling. When the announcement's made that the bus is boarding in five minutes, I look up from the newspaper in time to catch Paz through the plate glass window, and he's moving with determination. I wasn't just being paranoid before. Big Joe must've paid someone here at the bus depot to be looking for me.

If I try running Paz will shoot me down like a dog, so I do what he's not expecting me to do, which is fight back. I grab a lady's suitcase, and I move just as fast to the door as Paz is, and I hit him with the suitcase just as he's stepping through it. Then the two of us are on the floor grappling— me trying to keep him from pointing his gun at me, him trying to blow my head off.

I'm gasping in air as we wrestle. I'm able to slam his gun hand down hard enough to make him drop it, and I get the sense that the gun has scattered out of reach. It doesn't stop him from getting the upper hand on me and rolling onto my chest, his hands reaching for my throat, then squeezing it. I guess if he can't shoot me, he's going to choke me to death. I'm bucking and fighting, trying not to black out, but it seems hopeless with how my lungs feel like they're bursting and the way my vision's blurring. But then things change with him slumping over me. As blurry as my vision is, I can see the cops dragging Paz off me. Then two of them are pulling me to my feet, and being kind of rough about it.

The cops take me to the station and dump me in a small interrogation room. I decide I'm going to mostly tell the truth—that Big Joe has a grudge against me and sent Paz to kill me. I'll lie about what the grudge is about—maybe tell them that I slept with Big Joe's daughter and he found out about it. Let them prove otherwise. In the end they'll let me go. They'll be curious about the diamond ring and the almost thousand in my wallet, but they won't be able to prove its not mine, and in all the confusion the bag I had with the rest of the dough and the jewelry was left in the depot. By now someone slick must've picked it up and left town with it. So the cops have nothing to hold me on. Still, I'm surprised by how long they're keeping me waiting in this room. It must be hours by now.

When a cop who introduces himself as Detective Mark Foley finally comes to see me, I feign outrage, saying, "Vincent Paz went to the bus depot to kill me. I was only defending myself. You have no right sticking me in this room and forgetting about me like you did."

He doesn't answer me. He just sits across from me and places the diamond ring on the table in front of him.

"If you want me to, I'll tell you why Vincent Paz was sent to kill me—"

He interrupts me, telling me doesn't care about Vincent Paz. "What I want you to tell me is where you got this ring," he says. Something about his voice chills me.

"My dear old mom's. The only thing she left me when she died."

He smiles at that. "What was your mom's name?"

"Why?"

He shrugs. "I want to check her initials to what's engraved on the inside of the ring. I'm curious why her last name must be different from yours. So how about you tell me her name?"

I acted like an amateur never checking whether the ring was engraved. I say, "My pop bought the ring secondhand before he gave it to my mom. So what. It's the thought that counts, right?"

He doesn't challenge me about this. Instead he takes a photo from a folder and places it in front of me. I recognize the woman in the photo, and before I'm able to control my expression, he sees that I recognize her. It's the same woman in the snapshot Green had the diamond ring sitting on top of, except the photo the cop shows me is a morgue shot. I start getting a sick feeling in my gut, but what I'm thinking doesn't seem possible.

"Do you know her?"

I shake my head.

"It's funny that you don't know her since you had her ring."

I don't say anything. I can't.

"Where were you August eighth at one AM?"

August eighth was three weeks ago. That sick feeling is only getting worse. I already know what the answer is going to be, but I can't stop myself from asking him, "Why?"

"Because that's when you beat her to death and left her body in a vacant lot on the corner of Washington and Pine."

I had passed that same vacant lot when I went to the old man's house answering his caretaker ad. It's three blocks from Green's house. I'm stunned at how badly I had misjudged him. When I found the jewelry and photos, I thought they were trophies he had taken years ago from women he seduced and robbed. But that wasn't it. They were trophies all right, but they were trophies taken by a serial killer. Green must've murdered all those women. Even three weeks ago when I thought he was lying in bed an invalid he was sneaking out of the house and killing another woman. My head's swimming thinking how he had me groom him so he'd look his best when he killed more women.

Foley is waiting patiently for me to answer him, but what am I going to say? I can't tell him about Green, not after shooting him and burning down his house, and I have no alibi and no way of setting one up. I can't think of a single person who would vouch for me, not with Big Joe wanting my scalp. I realize it's as simple as my luck's run out, so I don't say another word. Not then, and not when I'm being booked. Maybe after I'm found guilty of murder and am sentenced I'll think of something to say, but even then I don't think I'll be able to.

SOME PEOPLE DESERVE TO DIE

Originally published in the August 2011 issue of Ellery Queen Mystery Magazine.

Dr. Jerry Herse was fitting a temporary crown over my root canal when I received a call about the murder. With my mouth filled with clamps and other dental instruments all I could do was grunt back a response to the precinct Captain. He wasn't particularly amused at my predicament and, rather sourly, gave me the address where the body was found, telling me to go over there as soon as I could. Which meant he wanted me there a half hour ago.

I sat impatiently for the next ten minutes while Dr. Herse removed the clamps and other junk from my mouth and wrote me a prescription for Percocet. For the time being I was numbed out enough with Novocain that the prescription could wait. I drove straight to the murder site; the third level of a parking garage near Kendall Square.

My partner, Joe Sullivan, was already there, as was our crime scene specialist and two of his interns. The crime scene specialist stopped what he was doing to nod to me, then continued taking pictures of the area. Joe and the interns were standing by an older model Honda Civic. Joe was in his late thirties; a big burly man with a scarred face and a flattened nose from his amateur boxing days. Joe "Red" Sullivan, at one time the pride of South Boston, although he had lost most of his reddish sandy hair since partnering with me so his old nickname didn't quite fit anymore. From the neighborhood Joe came from he could've easily turned criminal, but he went the other way and now had fourteen years of service in; me, I had twenty-six years. In another four if things went as planned, I'd be leaving Massachusetts and these lousy winters far behind to buy a bar in Key Biscayne after I had my thirty-year pension.

As I approached them, I spotted the body lying on the ground beyond the Honda. Male, late twenties, maybe early thirties, thin, medium height, dark complexion, probably of Indian descent, wearing worn jeans, a stained polo shirt, and dirty sneakers. The front part of his skull had been caved in above his right eye and a small puddle of blood had pooled by his head. I tried asking Joe what they had, but because of the damn Novocain my speech came out slurred. That brought a hard grin from my partner. I knew he'd be in a rotten mood—he'd been talking all week about going to the Bruins game tonight, and with the murder he now had little chance of using his tickets.

"Started drinking early today, huh, Steve?" he asked, an eyebrow arched innocently.

He knew I had a two o'clock appointment with my endodontist, and further that the last two weeks a lower molar of mine had abscessed and the pain from it left me popping Advil every hour. For the past two weeks it was as if nails were being hammered into my jaw. No relief—not for a second. The last few days while waiting for my appointment I had fantasized about pulling the damn thing out myself with a pair of pliers. Now the numbness I was experiencing was a godsend.

I gave him a long cold look. If my lower lip had any life in it I would've wished for him to experience the joy of an abscess and the accompanying root canal, but if I tried slurring that I would've cracked him up so instead I ignored his comment and kept up with the silent treatment. After a minute of that his grin faded.

"You look like hell, Steve," he said. "Lousy timing for a murder, huh? Root canal go okay?"

"Yeah, I feel like a million," I said, talking like a ventriloquist with palsy. "What do we got?"

Joe nodded towards the dead body. "Victim is one Sanjay Patel. The Honda Civic he's next to is registered to him. According to a work badge found on his person, he's employed at a software company on Broadway about two blocks from here. Can't say for sure until the ME examines him, but it looks like the cause of death was the blow he took to the temple. From the dent in his skull, he was whacked pretty good. Nothing else that's visible."

"One blow?"

"That would be my guess."

I squinted at the body. The damage to the skull looked extensive. If that was done by a single blow, whoever did it put a lot of muscle behind it. I shifted my gaze back to my partner. "ME's on the way?"

Joe nodded, chewing on his bottom lip impatiently. "Yeah, a call was put in over a half hour ago. He should've been here already."

While Cambridge is home to two major universities and is as congested as any urban setting, we don't get enough murders to justify having our own medical examiner—usually only one or two a year—so we rent out Boston's when we need the help.

"Joe, you might as well forget those hockey tickets. You're not going to be using them tonight."

My partner glared at me for a moment before nodding glumly. I noticed a tire iron that had been placed in a plastic evidence bag. There was something brownish-red caked on it. Already knowing the answer, I asked if that was the murder weapon.

"Yeah, looks like it. It was left next to the body." Joe paused for a moment to run a hand through the little hair he had left on his head. "It also looks like it was taken out of the victim's car. The tire iron's for the same model Honda Civic, and the one that should've been in the trunk is missing. Steve, this wasn't a robbery. Money and credit cards were left in the victim's wallet. I don't think anything was taken."

I gave the car another look. The windows were intact, as was the trunk. Whoever did this probably used a Slim Jim to unlock the front door, then pressed the trunk release to get at the tire iron. I asked one of the interns if they took fingerprints off the car yet. She told me they did. I turned to Joe and asked if he could open the trunk. He fished a set of keys from an evidence bag and pressed the remote button to pop the trunk open. The spare had been put back in place.

"This the way you found it?" I asked.

"Yep."

I studied the inside of the trunk, noting how neat and orderly it appeared. This was looking more and more like a professional job. Someone taking their time to remove the tire iron from under the spare, then putting everything back in order and waiting for the victim so he could kill him with one well-placed blow. An amateur would've left the trunk in disarray, and probably also would've hit the body a half-dozen more times before being satisfied that the man was dead. This was someone with ice-water in his veins; someone who knew exactly what he was doing.

I closed the trunk and felt a tightness contracting my stomach as I realized what we were up against. It was bad enough to have a murder in the city but having one you weren't going to be able to solve was far worse, and if the killer was as professional as he appeared I doubted we were going to solve it, at least not without a lucky break. A winning the lottery-type lucky break. I asked Joe who found the body.

"Patrolman Winston." Joe's lids lowered half-way giving him a tired, washed-out look. "Routine drive thru after last week's briefing. He spotted the body."

There had been a rash of car thefts the last few weeks from several of the garages around Central Square, and we were having patrolmen do some routine drive-throughs hoping to discourage it. If we had been able to get the garages to put security cameras up instead this murder would've had a good chance of already being solved. Patrolman Lou Winston was standing about a hundred feet away staring stone-faced at us. I waved him over and asked whether he saw anyone. He didn't. So far no witnesses either, which was about what I expected. The only thing he was able to tell me was he found the body at 3:18. I let him go back to stand vigil.

"What do you want to do?" Joe asked, again pushing a hand through his sparse hair. "Wait for the ME?"

"No reason to. We can see him later. Let's go talk to some of Patel's co-workers."

The murdered man's boss acted at first as if we pulling a gag on him. When it finally dawned on him that this was no joke, the color left his face leaving it a sickly white and I thought for a moment he was going to pass out. He collected himself, though, and a little color came back peppering his cheeks. He had no idea what time Patel left the office or why.

"Sanjay was very quiet," he said. "He mostly kept to himself."

"Any problems with co-workers?" Joe asked.

He was shaking his head, but paused midway, and shifted his gaze back to us. Still looking dazed, he told us how Patel was going through a divorce. "The little I've heard it was pretty ugly," he said.

Joe snuck me a look. An ugly divorce. That would explain a professional being involved. We talked some more, but other than that Patel had been working there three years we got nothing else from him. After that we talked with everyone else in the office. Some of them were shocked to hear about a co-worker being murdered, others didn't seem to care one way or the other, but the one thing they had in common was none of them had any personal relationship with Patel. We kept hearing the same comments about how Patel was quiet and kept to himself. A few of his co-workers who sat near him overheard recent conversations he'd had with his lawyer, and were able to piece together that he was going through a heated and very contentious divorce. One of his co-workers remembered seeing him red-faced and stewing after one of these conversations. When his co-worker, alarmed, asked Patel what was wrong, the dead man had muttered something about how his wife wasn't going to get a penny before turning back to his work. The only other thing we got from talking to any of them was from the software developer who sat across from Patel who remembered seeing Patel leave around two-thirty. Before we left, Patel's boss was able to give us the last contact number he had for the dead man's wife. He let us use a speaker phone in one of their conference rooms. It turned out the number was for her cell phone and she was at work at an accounting firm in downtown Boston. She sounded surprised to hear from us. When she asked why we were calling, we told her it would be better if we explained in person. She complained that she needed to leave work soon, but Joe warned her that it would be better if she stayed put where she was, then hung up.

We had a cell phone that Joe had found on Patel's belt. Most of the outgoing calls were for the same number and when Joe tried it he ended up reaching Patel's lawyer. Joe talked for a while, then after hanging up told me how the guy's attitude changed quickly after he found out his client was dead. "He seemed pretty pissed off," Joe said, his eyes glistening with amusement, a smirk hardening his lips. "I guess Patel owes him a bundle in fees; money he's now got a prayer's chance in hell of ever seeing."

"He's going to make himself available to us?" I asked.

"Yep. He works on Tremont Street near Park Station. He's going to hang around and meet us at the Parker House lounge after we talk to the widow."

I nodded. It was already past five. Some feeling had already come back to my lower lip. It was sore, kind of a dull ache, but nowhere near the excruciating pain I'd been suffering before the root canal. With some luck I wouldn't have to be popping Percocet over the next few days. Anyway, it was a relief to have that tooth dead and the pain gone. I opened my mouth wide and moved my jaw from side to side, feeling as if I'd be able to talk normally. At least I'd no longer look as if I was in the middle of having a stroke.

It was five-twenty before I was able to navigate through Boston traffic and park in front of the building where the widow worked. She was waiting for us in the accounting firm's lobby. A small, thin woman with unbelievably dark eyes. She reminded me of a wounded bird, a sparrow, and might've been attractive if her face wasn't so tense and anxious. She stared from Joe to me, fear mixing in with the anxiety.

"I was supposed to leave a half hour ago to pick up my son," she said, trying hard to force some anger in her voice. "He's at daycare now, and they'll be charging me extra for this. What lies are my husband saying about me?"

"Excuse me," I asked, trying hard to look sympathetic while at the same time sizing her up. The odds were she was the one who put a pro on her husband. Along with the fake show of anger there was plenty of fear in her face. I decided to play it straight. "Your husband was found murdered in a parking garage near where he worked. That's why we're here."

She blinked at me several times, her eyes turning glassy, and then she stumbled backwards until she could sit down. She reached blindly behind to feel for the chair.

"Oh my God," she muttered mostly to herself. She seemed in shock, but then again even if it was genuine, it could be nothing more than seeing the murder she had put in play go from abstract concept to reality.

"We need to ask you some questions." Joe told her, his manner blunt.

She looked up at him dazed. Slowly some intelligence filtered into her dark eyes. "You think I had something to do with this," she said.

"Ma'am, I didn't imply anything of the kind," Joe answered back with a straight face.

"Of course you did," she snapped, her mouth twisting into something bitter. "You heard about our divorce and thought I could do something like this."

"Mrs. Patel," I said. "This is all routine. We have to question you."

She turned towards me. Her eyes were now fully alive.

"I hated Sanjay," she told me. "He was a horrible man. Cheap and mean. But it would make no sense for me to want him dead, at least not now. He stole everything we had and moved the money to his parents in Bangalore. It didn't matter to him that he was leaving me and my son penniless. My lawyer was making him give a full accounting so that the judge would make him return our money. If I were going to kill him it would be after that."

"We still need to talk with you," Joe said.

"No, not now. Now I need to pick up my son. If you want to talk you can come by my apartment later." Her eyes blazed for a moment as she stared hotly at Joe. "But if you want to talk to who killed Sanjay, talk to his parents. They are cheap like him. They would do anything to keep our money from being returned."

"How much money are we talking about?" I asked.

She looked back at me almost as if she had forgotten I was there. "Over two hundred thousand dollars," she said, spitting out the words as if they were poison. "Along with all of our savings, Sanjay took out a ninety-three thousand dollar second mortgage on our condo. He would've gone back home to India except my lawyer convinced the judge to make Sanjay give up his passport."

That last part was said with some vindication. I told her to give me her address and we would talk to her later that night. Joe flashed me a look as if I was nuts, but I ignored him and had Mrs. Patel write out her home address for me. I watched as she stood up and walked out of the office, her legs shaky. Joe waited until she was out of sight before telling me we should've taken her in. I shook my head and told him she had a kid in daycare to pick up.

"You buy her story?"

"Enough of it," I said. "Maybe not about the parents hiring a hit man from two continents away, but I think I'd like to talk to Patel's lawyer first and find out how much of what she told us was true."

He mumbled something about how the Novocain must've reached my brain, but he had the same doubts I did, otherwise he would've insisted we bring the wife in for further questioning. It was more than just doubt on my part, though. I knew if we brought her in she'd be lawyering up before we got another word out of her. I could see it in those dark eyes of hers. This way we'd have a chance to talk to her some more without a lawyer shutting us down.

While we drove to meet Patel's lawyer, the ME returned a call I had made earlier. He told me the victim died from massive hemorrhaging and that death had been pretty much instantaneous. "He was probably dead before he hit the ground," the ME added.

"Just the single blow to the temple?"

"Just the one."

"What's the chance of being hit like that and surviving?"

"With the force that was used? Same as Bluto's grade point average."

"What?"

"Zero point zero."

"Yeah, okay," I said, feeling a bit dense for not more quickly making the connection to the Animal House reference. After all, I'd only seen the movie a dozen times, but taking Joe's clue from earlier, I blamed it on the aftereffects of the Novocain. "Were you able to narrow down time of death?"

He paused at that, hemming and hawing a bit before telling me how since the victim was seen leaving his workplace at two-thirty and his body discovered at three-eighteen, that that probably narrowed it down as well as he could.

We talked for a while longer, mostly shooting the bull, but the ME had nothing much at that time to add. Just that he was able to identify the tire iron as the murder weapon, that Patel appeared to be a healthy thirty-two year-old male before being fatally struck on the temple with that same tire iron, and that in his opinion the blow was meant to kill. When I pulled up to the Parker House, I thanked him for the callback and filled Joe in on what was said, or at least what he wasn't able to piece together from listening to my end of the conversation.

Patel's lawyer was waiting for us inside the Parker House lounge as promised, sitting at the bar with a half-finished martini. A lot of other guys in suits who could also be lawyers were sitting at the bar with him, but we were able to identify him by calling his cell phone and seeing which of the suits answered. The suit that answered was an expensive one—probably a grand easy, and the guy wearing it was in his late thirties and built like a fireplug. Something made him look over his shoulder. He spotted us and, from our cheap suits, quickly made the connection as to who we were. He took his half-finished martini with him as he got up from the bar to meet us.

"You must be the detectives who called me earlier about Sanjay," he said, introducing himself as Martin Gould, and first offering his free hand to Joe, then to me. "Why don't we grab a table back there where it's quiet and we can talk."

We let him lead the way. Once we were seated he drained what was left of his martini and waved a waitress over so he could order another one. Joe ordered a beer and a pub burger. The Novocain had completely worn off at this point and the area around my dead tooth felt achy and sore. I ordered a double-scotch, and not thinking I could handle solid food, asked for a bowl of clam chowder.

"It's the only chance we're going to have to eat tonight," I explained to Gould. He looked bemused at that explanation, but didn't bother to mention anything about the alcoholic drinks we both ordered.

"Sanjay was murdered, huh?" he said, shaking his head. "So how can I help you fellows?"

"We heard it was a pretty ugly divorce," Joe said.

Gould nodded. "That would be an accurate way to characterize it."

"The wife told us herself she hated her husband."

"Not hard to believe"

"You think she could be involved?"

A hard smile pulled at Gould's lips giving him a bulldog look. "Not a chance," he said.

"Why not?"

Gould looked at us hesitantly for a moment before a shadow fell over his eyes. Grim-faced, he made up his mind to talk about his dead client.

"Sanjay Patel was a piece of work," he said. "He bullied and terrorized his wife for the duration of their marriage and at this point I'm sure all she wanted was to be free of him; well, that and getting some of her money back. If you spoke with her she must've told you about how he sent all the money they had to India. With him now dead it's going to be near impossible for her to get any of that back. Me, I'm going to have to kiss nearly thirty thousand in legal fees good bye."

The waitress returned with our drinks. Gould picked the olive out of his martini and popped it in his mouth, then lifted his glass. "Here's to clients who have the decency to pay their bills before getting bumped off," he said somewhat whimsically.

"The wife told us he transferred over two hundred grand," Joe said.

Gould thought about it, nodded. "That sounds about right. He moved their money regularly over the last four years emptying out everything they had, then before filing for a divorce he took all the equity out of their condo through a second mortgage and moved that also."

"Where's the money now?"

"Most likely with his parents in India. Her lawyer is in the middle of a discovery motion, and is trying to get an accounting of those funds."

"This money transfer went on for four years?" I asked.

"Yep. She didn't have a clue about it, though."

"How's that?"

He took a long sip of his martini, his eyes dulling as they lifted and met mine. "He had her completely in the dark about their finances, and for the most part about everything. He isolated her from her family, and used her as a workhorse to finance his new life in India. Or what would've been his new life if someone hadn't called her lawyer to tip him off. If that hadn't happen and the courts hadn't forced him to surrender his passport, I'm sure he'd be back in India now."

"Sounds like his wife had good reason to hate him," I said. "Sometimes hate is a stronger motivation for murder than money."

He shook his head. "It's not in her. Not from what I could see. The woman's a lamb, Sanjay was the wolf."

"She had some crazy idea that his parents could be behind this," Joe muttered half under his breath.

Gould thought about that, nodded. "It's not that crazy. Sanjay was cut from the same cloth as those two, and it wouldn't surprise me if they'd do something like that."

"Did you ever speak to them?"

"Once," he said. "I tried to explain to them what could happen if they refused to send back the money, but they seemed more concerned about ways they could hide the money than their son's welfare."

Joe's burger and my clam chowder were brought over. Gould asked the waitress for the check, then finished his martini and pushed himself away from the table.

"Dinner's on me, detectives," he said. "Enjoy."

"Thanks. Any idea who tipped off the wife's lawyer about the money transfers?" I asked.

He smiled grimly. "Probably someone who didn't want to see his dirt bag client get away with stealing two hundred thousand dollars and leaving an innocent woman and her two year-old child destitute. Any other questions, feel free to call me anytime."

He left and both Joe and I half-heartedly ate our food. It was looking like we had legitimate suspects two continents away, and the thought of that wasn't helping our appetites.

"This is going to be a mess," Joe grumbled.

I agreed with him and thought hard about ordering another double-scotch, but we still had a long night ahead of us, even without trying to figure out how to get authorities in India involved.

Later that night we met again with the widow at her apartment, a small one-bedroom in Everett. She explained how her husband had left her buried in debt and this was all she could afford.

"What type of man would make his own son live like this?" she asked.

I couldn't answer her. Her son looked small for his age, but had these huge brown eyes and stared fixated up at Joe. Joe had never married and didn't have any kids of his own, and I couldn't help smiling seeing how this attention from a two-old boy unnerved him so much. Mrs. Patel was also tense, her eyes moving from Joe to me like ping pong balls, but she seemed to relax a bit when we asked for contact information for her dead husband's parents. I guess she realized we were taking her earlier suggestion seriously. We asked her some more perfunctory questions, but didn't get anything that made it look like she was involved. She was nervous because we were cops, nothing more. She gave us her dead husband's last address. Neither of them had been living in their condo. According to her it was under foreclosure.

"Before the divorce he was supposed to be paying the mortgage," she said, some wetness showing around her eyes. "But he didn't. For six months he didn't. Instead the money was sent to his parents. Right after he moved out I received the foreclosure notices. He ruined my credit so badly, I was lucky to be able to rent this apartment. I had to pay them four months' rent in advance to get it. What type of man would do that to his wife and child?"

Again, all I could so was shake my head.

"A cheap man," she said. She started crying then, the floodgates opening up. "A cheap and horrible man"

The boy started crying in sympathy. I could see Joe desperately wanted to bail, but I couldn't do that. I sat next to her and put my arm around her, and felt her shrink into herself. The boy buried himself into Joe's pant leg. Joe glared daggers at me, but I ignored him and waited until Mrs. Patel stopped crying.

Sanjay Patel's studio apartment in Somerville looked like the place of someone who wasn't going to be there long. Outside of a card table near the kitchen for him to eat his food on and a mattress on the floor there was no other furniture. There wasn't much in there other than a laptop, some clothes and papers scattered about, and it took less than fifteen minutes to search the place. It was at the bottom of a garbage bag that I found the magazine where an advertisement in the back pages had been circled. The ad was for a special type of troubleshooter who could take care of difficult problems. From the type of magazine I expected to find a lot of ads like that, and it didn't surprise me that one of them was circled. The only contact information in the ad was for a P.O. Box in Revere. I called Joe over to show him what I found.

"Son of a bitch," he said.

"Yeah."

"He was going to have his wife killed."

"Yeah."

"It backfired on him. Got him killed instead."

"That's what it looks like."

"Son of a bitch."

Joe stood frozen, his face reddening with anger. "I missed the Bruins game for this guy…"

He was too mad to finish what he was going to say. We left the apartment together and found the nearest bar where we could catch the third period of the game on TV. I bought the first few rounds while Joe sat stewing. It didn't help that the Bruins lost.

We staked out the UPS Store where the P.O. Box was located for three weeks before I spotted our man. The FBI had sent me a dossier on known hit men who worked the area, and I recognized Mike Nelson as soon as he walked into the store. He was a big man with thick arms and dead eyes. He took several steps towards his mailbox, but some sort of sixth sense alerted him that I was there because he turned on his heels and walked out of the place before he could open his mailbox and pick up the letter I had sent him answering his ad.

I stayed where I was and gave Joe a call. He was parked outside, and he had made our hit man also. He called me back five minutes later to tell me our guy was sitting in a bar only three doors down.

"How do you want to play this?" he asked.

We could continue the stakeout, but this had been going on three weeks, and I didn't think Nelson would be using that P.O. Box again. And I knew why he was waiting where he was.

"I'm going to talk to him," I said. "Probably best if I do it alone."

Joe didn't argue with me. He told me he'd be parked out front of the bar waiting for me.

Three doors down was a place called Maguire's. Joe was double-parked out in front of it. Inside sitting at a back table was Mike Nelson. He stared at with me with pale dead eyes before nodding.

"Detective," he said. "Why don't you take a seat."

I sat across from him.

"What are you drinking?" he asked.

He had some murky brown liquid in a shot glass in front of him. I told him scotch, and he indicated that to the bartender.

"I hope I didn't keep you waiting long," I said.

"No, not too long."

"How'd you know I was watching your box?"

He smiled, but it was as dead as his eyes. "Don't know what you're talking about, Detective."

"If you're not going to answer any questions, then what's the point of this?"

He smiled again, but it remained as lifeless as before. "Detective, I'm having this psychic flash that you're investigating a homicide. How does that sound?"

I didn't answer him. His eyes stayed locked on mine.

"Why don't you tell me which murder you're investigating?"

He knew which one, but he wanted me to tell him, so I did.

"Yeah, I remember reading about that in the papers," he said. "Hypothetically speaking, why would I want to kill this Patel guy, assuming I'm not the sweet and gentle guy that I am."

"Let's quit these games. I've seen your FBI dossier."

He raised an eyebrow at that. "I'm not admitting to anything. But hypothetically, if I was a hit man and I killed this Patel, you'd never find any evidence tying me to it, so Detective, you'd be wasting your time sitting here talking to me."

"Why wouldn't I be able to tie you to it?"

He made a face as if he'd tasted something unpleasant. "If I remember right from what I read in the papers there were no surveillance cameras where this Patel was killed and no witnesses. If you had any physical evidence tying me to his murder, I'm sure you'd be arresting me now instead of sitting here with me. So it seems obvious. But I'm talking hypothetically, of course, 'cause I'm not a hit man. Just a guy sitting in a bar indulging one of Cambridge's finest."

Of course he was right. We had no witnesses, no physical evidence, no money links, nothing except a circled magazine ad, and that was no longer going to do us any good unless we could find one of Nelson's fingerprints on the mailbox, which I doubted was a possibility.

My scotch was brought over. I took it in one gulp, then found myself shaking my head.

"Why?" I heard myself asking.

He looked at me confused.

"Why kill your client?" I asked. "What happened, did Patel try to stiff you? Did he try blackmailing you into doing the murder for free? Why kill him?"

Nelson scratched his jaw, thinking about what I had asked. "This is all hypothetical," he said. "Just stuff I'm piecing together from what I read in the papers." He stopped for a moment, probably trying to figure out how to word things so it couldn't be used as a confession. "Let's say hypothetically I was a hit man and someone like Patel hired me, and let's say this guy pays me everything he owes me, not without a lot of moaning about it, but he pays me, and then he tells me he wants his wife dead 'cause of all the money he stole from her, not because he gives a rat's ass about his two-year old boy, that he's actually thinking of selling his son to a pedophile before he heads back to India so he doesn't have to be stuck taking care of him. Maybe he actually has the gall to ask me if I know anyone who might be interested."

"That's what he asked you? To help him sell his son to a

pedophile?"

"This is all hypothetical," Nelson stated with a stubborn insistence. "Nothing more than how I'd imagine this conversation might have gone. And maybe in this imaginary hypothetical conversation his exact words might've been that he wanted to sell his son to someone who could make use of him, but it would be pretty damn obvious what he meant by that, wouldn't it?"

A wave of anger flushed Nelson's face, and he lowered his eyes and cleared his throat to better compose himself, then those dead eyes were back on mine. "Let's just say some people deserve to die," he said in a soft voice.

"Thank you."

The words just slipped out of me. He gave me a puzzled look, as if he were uncertain whether I was thanking him for answering my question or for killing Patel. To be honest, I didn't know the answer to that myself. I felt shaky as I got up from the table and walked out of the bar. I thought about what Patel asked of Nelson and doubted that Patel was really looking to sell his son to a pedophile. Maybe he didn't care if that's where his son ended up, but it probably didn't matter to him for what purpose his son was sold—whether it was to a couple who wanted a child, or to be raised as a domestic servant. I was glad, though for the misunderstanding. Without it, Nelson might not have been incensed enough to change his target.

When I got in the car next to Joe, he gave me a concerned look. "Jesus, you look like you just saw a ghost. What happened in there?" he asked.

"Nothing," I said. "I hit a dead end, nothing more than that." I paused for a moment as I made a decision. "We might as well go back to the station house and tell the Captain we've run out of leads. He's not going to like it, but we're wasting our time on this."

Joe grimaced thinking about it. "There's got to be something we can do," he said. "I mean, come on, at least we know who the hit man is."

UNLUCKY SEVEN

I could have explained the simple truth; that as Nelson so eloquently put it some people just deserve to die, but Joe was a black and white kind of guy, he didn't see gray areas well. I didn't bother saying anything, and we rode back to the station house in silence.

A GUILTY CONSCIENCE

My partner Joe Sullivan wasn't happy. I would've known that even if I hadn't heard him grinding his teeth or caught a glimpse of him brooding as he maneuvered the car through East Cambridge traffic. But then again, I wasn't happy either, and I didn't bother answering him when he complained about how we'd better catch a break soon. I couldn't disagree with him. We both knew that time was running out for Danielle Wells, a tiny seven year-old girl who was all skinny legs and arms and thick, tangled brown hair, and who went missing four days ago. The photos her parents gave us had her wearing a yellow party dress with her hair tied up in a ponytail. It wasn't her brown eyes that got to me as much as her smile. The thought that we might not find her in time was a stab to the heart, especially whenever I pictured the shy, awkward smile that she showed in those photos.

We both sat stewing in our thoughts while we inched along Cambridge Street. Joe interrupted the silence by grumbling that we should be calling these people instead of driving out so we could interview them face to face. "None of these jokers are going to know a damn thing," he complained under his breath. "Walsh is just wasting our time."

Captain Jack Walsh was our precinct captain. Here I disagreed with Joe, and although I didn't say anything to him about it, I thought Walsh had a valid point in wanting us to visit each person calling the hotline that was set up for little Danielle. The other lines of inquiry had turned ice cold, and this was all we had. Maybe ninety-nine out of a hundred citizens calling knew nothing useful, but it was that hundredth guy we needed to find, and if we had eyes on that person when we spoke to him, we'd have a better idea when we found him.

To say that traffic had slowed down to a crawl would've been generous. I was staring out the windshield and didn't have Joe in my peripheral vision, but I could sense his irritation flaring up, so it didn't surprise me when he flipped on the police lights and swung the car into the oncoming lane, and it was only by a minor miracle that a gray Ford Fiesta avoided us without crashing up. I kept my mouth shut. One look at how beet-red Joe's neck had turned and I knew better than to give him any grief. Later I would, but not right then. It was only after he was able to turn off Cambridge Street onto Eighth with everyone unscathed and no property damage having occurred that I let out my breath. Joe took three more side streets, and two minutes later he pulled up to the small white Colonial where Dennis Lange lived.

Given that Joe's ears had turned redder than his neck, I knew he was steaming, and I also knew it was mostly over the accident he almost caused on Cambridge Street. I wisely swallowed back a crack about how Joe 'Red' Sullivan had made a reappearance—which was the moniker given to him when he was boxing in South Boston at the age of nineteen thanks to the color of his hair, most of which was now gone and the little that was left no longer red. Again, I would save that crack for later.

We both got out of the car. Lange's house was typical of East Cambridge: a small Colonial squeezed between two nearly identical Colonials with narrow cement alleys separating the houses, and a front yard barely big enough to fit two bodies buried side by side. An older model Chevy station wagon filled up the small driveway, so Lange was most likely at home. Something I found odd was that it was a quarter past three in the afternoon and all the window shades were drawn. I pointed that out to Joe. His eyes deadened as he gave the house a cold stare.

"He's also got cardboard covering his basement windows," Joe said.

I had missed that. "I guess the man likes his privacy."

"It must be something like that."

I felt my pulse quicken. From the hardness that had settled over my partner's features, I knew Joe was thinking the same as me: that there was something very wrong here. As we made our way to the front door, a window shade was pushed aside. I didn't have to point it out to Joe. A glint in his eyes showed that he had seen it also.

It didn't take long after I rang the bell for a man who I assumed was Lange to answer the door. He was in his late sixties, on the short side, with a round body, an equally round head, and a sickly, pale complexion. Instead of sticking his head out and asking us who we were, or possibly inviting us in, he opened the door just enough so he could squeeze through the opening, and then closed the door shut behind him to keep us from looking inside.

"You must be here because of me calling about that little girl?" he asked, a nervous hitch showing along the side of his mouth.

As he stood blinking in the sunlight, I decided his complexion looked more washed out than pale. My attention was drawn to his milk-white doughy hands, which were maybe the whitest hands I'd ever seen, but what struck me even more than those hands were his large bulging eyes, which made me think of an ageing Peter Lorre.

"My name's Detective Heller and this is Detective Sullivan," I said. "We have a few questions for you."

He did a double take as he looked at Joe, almost as if he had seen a ghost, and then turned a confused face to me.

"I don't understand why you're here. When I called the hotline, I told the operator everything I know."

"We appreciate your calling but we have some follow-up questions we need to ask you," I said.

Joe started to say something, but before he could get the question out, Lange turned toward him. "I knew you looked familiar," he said, his bug-eyed look unchanged. "Joe 'Red' Sullivan. I saw you in the ring maybe twenty years ago. At the Garden. You gave the guy a pretty good beating if I remember right." He forced a thin smile. "You had more hair then, but then again, didn't we all?"

"How about us continuing this inside," I said, drawing his attention back to me.

"I'm okay out here," Lange said. "The fresh air will do me some good. Go ahead, ask me what you need to ask me."

"You could do us a big favor," Joe said, showing a toothy smile while trying hard to turn on the charm, which wasn't something that came naturally with him. "Me and my partner have been dogging it all day and could use some coffee. How about we step inside and you make us some, and I'll tell you all about that fight at the Garden while the coffee's brewing."

"I don't have any coffee inside. There's a Dunkin' Donuts a block away. It will be my treat, and I got no problem with us talking there."

"You seem to not want us inside your house. It's making us think you've got something to hide," I said.

His jaw fell slack as he looked at me. "What are you talking about?"

"Come on, Dennis," Joe said, friendly-like. "Look at it from our perspective. You call us up about a missing girl and we find all your window shades pulled down and your basement windows cardboarded up. You've got to admit that's going to look funny to us. How about you let us look around inside your house so we can feel good about you?"

He was shaking his head, flustered, his complexion dropping to a color you might see on a dead fish. "I put cardboard up over those casement windows for insulation, no other reason. And I don't like people in my house."

"Why not?"

He glared at me, some anger peppering his cheeks. "I don't have to explain myself to you! Jesus, I called up that hotline because I was worried about that girl and saw something that I thought might help, and you start accusing me of stuff!"

"We're not accusing you of anything," Joe said. "But you got to understand how this looks to us. If you give us five minutes to look inside your home we can clear this up, and we can then go over what you saw so we can save Danielle. That's what we all want, right?"

"I'm not letting you in my house! I have my reasons!" Lange's eye dropped from Joe's, and he bit his lower lip as if he were about to make a confession. "I suffer from mysophobia," he said, his mouth weakening. "If I let you or anyone else in my home I'll have to spend weeks scrubbing the floors and walls before I'll be able to feel comfortable again in there." Tears wetted his eyes as he added, "This isn't right. I called because I wanted to help, and this is the way you're going to treat me?"

I took out a notepad and made a show of consulting it before turning a hard stare toward Lange. "You told the hotline operator you saw a suspicious white van driving down Otis Street. You don't give us a license plate or any other description other than the driver's in his forties and has dark hair. Otis Street is three miles from where we believe Danielle was grabbed, and you claim you saw this mysterious van a day before the abduction happened. How is this supposed to help us?"

"I'm not saying it will, but I had a funny feeling about that driver," Lange claimed. "It was the way he kept slowing down as if he were looking for a child to take."

"He could've been slowing down to look for an

address."

"That wasn't what he was doing." Lange's mouth clamped shut and his eyes glazed as if he were seeing something a thousand miles away. This lasted only a few seconds, and then he was back to giving me his bugged-eyed stare. "I know that from the way he looked away from me when he caught me looking at him." His eyelids lowered in an embarrassed sort of way and he shifted his stare away from me. "I'd seen that same look before. I should've written down his license plate number because I knew something bad was going to happen."

"What do you mean by that?"

His mouth crumbled for a moment. "Like I told you, I'd seen it before," he said.

"When was this?"

"Twenty-seven years ago. When that boy was taken."

My heart skipped a beat. "Andrew Meyer?" I asked.

Lange nodded, his eyes squeezing shut. "The same morning that boy was taken, I was walking on Spring Street and a car slowed down when it passed me like that van did. When I saw the look in the driver's eyes I knew something was wrong, and it has haunted me ever since that I didn't call the police about what I saw. That's why I called this time. I didn't want to be haunted again."

I felt a stillness in my head as I stared at Lange. Andrew Meyer was ten years old when he went missing. His abduction could very well have happened on Spring Street since the boy's family lived only a block away on Thorndike. My voice sounded odd to me as I asked him to tell me what he saw that day twenty-seven years ago.

"It's what I told you. A car slowed down on Spring Street as if the driver were looking for somebody. When I saw that look in his eyes it was like I had caught him in the act of doing something terrible, and it spooked me. Later when I heard about that Meyer boy disappearing, I knew it had to be that driver, but I never did anything about it. I didn't think anyone would believe me."

"Are you saying it was the same driver who took both children?"

"No, I didn't say anything like that. The driver back then was in his forties, just like the one I called the hotline about. But the look in their eyes was the same."

I asked Lange to describe the man who he thought might have taken Andrew Meyer and the car he was driving. Lange shook his head.

"How am I supposed to do that? It was too many years ago, and it's too fuzzy in my mind now. I didn't get a good enough look at him so that I could describe him. When I caught that look in his eyes I didn't want to look at him any longer. All I can remember about his car is that it was dark green and some sort of sedan." His mouth convulsed as if he were tasting something bitter. "It wasn't right the way you treated me."

Joe had been standing silently by while I questioned Lange about what he knew regarding Andrew Meyer, and he stopped me from pressing Lange any further by apologizing for the way I had acted.

"Detective Koss has been way out of line with the way he's treated you," Joe said. "The Cambridge Police Department appreciates you calling the hotline and helping us the way you did." Joe handed him a card with his contact information, and asked Lange to call if he remembered anything else.

As Lange stared at the card, his lips curled to show the insult he had suffered. "I hope what I told you helps you find that girl," he said in a dispirited voice, and then he disappeared back inside his house.

My legs felt heavier than usual as we made our way back to the car. Once we were inside it, I told Joe where we messed up was having him play the *good* cop. "It's just not a natural role for you," I explained.

Joe didn't respond to my dig. Instead he sat brooding sullenly, a darkness muddling his face. This lasted about a minute, and during this time I was lost in my own thoughts about Andrew Meyer and Danielle Wells. Andrew Meyer's abduction happened during my first year on the job. I was a patrolman then, and my only involvement in the case was helping the detectives canvas for witnesses. Still, though, the boy's abduction weighed heavily on all of us in the department. Nothing ever broke with the case, and Andrew was never found. The parents left the state ten years ago without ever finding out what happened to their son.

Joe broke out of his brooding by stating that Lange has Danielle inside his house.

"Maybe."

"Uh uh. No maybes about it. Danielle's in there. It's not enough that he grabbed her, that fat little sicko is getting his jollies playing with us. That was a load of crap he fed you."

A heavy weariness washed through me. I raised a hand to my eyes and slowly rubbed them. I couldn't disagree with what Joe was saying.

"I'll go back to the station and talk to Walsh and the ADA about a search warrant. Why don't you talk to the neighbors, see if anyone has anything they can give us. Maybe one of them knows when he cardboarded up those basement windows." Without any hope that it would be the case, I added, "Maybe one of them might've even seen something the day Danielle was taken."

"Steve, she could still be alive. We need to get inside that house."

What Joe was really saying was he didn't have any faith we'd get anything from Lange's neighbors, so we needed to make up a story to justify forcing our way into his house. I wasn't about to agree to that. Not yet, anyway. It wasn't because I was only two years away from my pension and didn't want to risk losing it. If I thought Danielle was still alive, I'd go along with what Joe wanted to do, but I didn't think there was any chance of that, at least not if Lange was the one who took her. I wasn't about to do anything that would let Lange escape a murder conviction because of an illegal search.

"We'll try it my way," I said, my voice sounding almost as weary as I felt.

I met with Walsh and the ADA assigned to the case, Mark Caplan, and told them about Lange. Caplan stared at me as if I was telling him a bad joke. "There's not a judge in the city who'll issue a search warrant because you found Lange squirrely," he said.

"What about him putting cardboard up over his basement windows?"

"You're kidding, right? He gave you his reason for that."

"Okay, so instead you've got his inane story about why he called the hotline. Because he saw a predatory look in a driver's eye? And he saw that same look twenty-seven years ago the same day Andrew Meyer was taken? This guy is having fun playing games with us."

"Thanks to that pesky fourth amendment, you don't get a search warrant because of a gut feeling."

"Danielle Wells is there, Mark. I know she is. If you get me a warrant we might be able to get to her while she's still alive."

Caplan gave me an impatient, fed-up look. "Does this Lange guy have any previous arrests? Complaints from neighbors? Anything?"

I shook my head. "He's clean. He's been careful, but I have no doubt that this is something he's been planning for a while."

Caplan stood up. As far he was concerned he was done wasting his time with me. "Give me something tangible. Even if it's flimsy as hell," he said, and he left the room.

Walsh was leaning back in his chair, his fingers interlaced as his hands rested on his stomach. He looked at me with concern. "Steve, you don't look too good," he said.

"I'm fine, just tired."

He nodded. He knew the toll Danielle Wells' disappearance was taking on us. "How sure are you that he's the guy?" he asked.

"Ninety-nine percent."

"Then keep digging. And keep Joe from getting us in trouble."

I told him I'd do my best.

An idea struck me while I was driving back to East Cambridge. After a few phone calls, I hit pay dirt, at least in a way, and several minutes later caught a glimpse of myself in the rearview mirror. I hadn't realized I'd been smiling, even if it was only in a bleak sort of way.

When I caught up with Joe he filled me in on what he had learned about Lange from his neighbors, which was that none of them knew anything about him.

"They don't talk to him, he doesn't talk to them. None of them have been in his home, and he hasn't been in any of theirs. As far as they're concerned he's just some creepy dude who's been in the neighborhood forever."

"Any of them see anything the day Danielle was taken, or since?"

He didn't answer me directly. Instead he spent a few seconds rubbing the back of his neck as if it were stiff. "There's a woman across the street who I think might want to help," he said, his eyes a blank slate as they met mine. "If we talk to her right, I think she'll give us what we need."

"We're not doing that."

"Jesus, Steve, that little girl still might be alive. We still got a chance to save her."

Joe no longer sounded convinced of that. I think it must've dawned on him like it did me that if Lange had taken Danielle, there wasn't any real chance of her being alive.

"I made some calls and we caught a break," I said. "Garbage collection is scheduled for Lange's street tomorrow morning. Maybe we'll get lucky and he'll take out his garbage tonight. If not, we'll wait until tomorrow."

We needed to keep an eye on Lange, but we didn't want him walking outside and spotting either me or Joe watching his house. If he did, he might think twice about bringing out his garbage for collection. I called Walsh and arranged to have another detective handle the stakeout. Not that it meant I was going to get any sleep that night. I knew there wasn't any chance of it, so instead I stayed at the station in case anything broke.

At six-thirty the following morning, Lange carried out three cans full of garbage and left them at the curb. Five minutes after he was back inside his home, the garbage was bagged up and on its way back to the precinct. Fifteen minutes later, Joe, myself, and two other detectives were sifting through it. Not much after that we found a receipt that showed Lange had bought two sixty pound bags of cement the day after Danielle went missing. It was grim, although not unexpected. The only slight consolation from that discovery was knowing that there was nothing we could've done to save Danielle, and that our waiting until morning didn't matter. Forty-five minutes after finding the receipt we had a signed warrant to search Lange's house and to dig up his basement.

Lange had a fit when we served him the warrant and he tried to bar us from his home, and we had to physically restrain him. Joe led a team to search the upstairs of the house, while I led a team into the basement.

The basement was set up as a storage area and a separate walled-in boiler room. When we moved boxes that were stacked in a corner of the storage part of the basement, we found a five foot by three foot section of the floor that had been replaced with new cement. Inside the boiler room, there was a pick and other tools that Lange must've used to break up his cement floor and dig a grave for Danielle Wells. He also had stacked the broken pieces of his old cement floor in there. When I searched a little further, I found the empty cement bags hidden behind the cement pieces. Lange might've been careless with the receipt, but he was smart enough to hide those bags.

We had brought a jackhammer to break up the cement floor, and while that was being done, I got a call from Walsh.

I moved into the boiler room so I could better hear him.

"We found Danielle," Walsh told me. "She's in rough shape, but she's alive, and expected to recover. Your guy Lange turned out to be a reliable witness. The scumbag who took Danielle is in his forties and has a white van, just like Lange told you."

I felt a throbbing in the back of my head that matched the jackhammer that was busting up the floor in the other part of the basement. Every instinct I had told me Lange was our guy. How could I be this wrong? For a long moment I stood frozen with the cell phone pressed against my ear, unable to think of what to say.

"Steve, did you hear what I told you? Danielle Wells has been found. Call off the search and bring everyone back to the station."

"Captain, there's too much noise here. I can't hear a word you're saying. I'll call you back."

I turned off the phone and went back to watch them finish breaking up the new cement that had been laid out. It didn't take long after that to find the buried remains of a ten year-old boy. I would've thought after twenty-seven years buried in the dirt that only Andrew Meyer's bones would've been left, but more of him had been preserved, and he was still wearing the same clothes he had on when he was taken. I called Walsh back and told him what we found.

I told Joe about Danielle before we arrested Lange. Neither of us spoke while we drove a handcuffed Lange back to the precinct for booking. It was partly because neither of us felt like talking with Lange in the backseat, and partly because we both had to process what had happened. Lange had told us the truth, at least as much as he was capable of, and he really did call the hotline because he was trying to help us save Danielle. He had recognized that evil, predatory look in that other driver's eyes because he had seen it before. Of course, he had lied about where he had seen it, but I had no doubt that he had seen it many times in the reflection of a mirror. I wondered why he felt so compelled to dig up his basement floor after he heard about Danielle's abduction, and I decided it was because he wasn't sure anymore whether he had really stolen and murdered Andrew Meyer all those years ago. Maybe he had convinced himself that it was all only a bad dream. Or maybe it was something else entirely. I almost asked him his reason, but a glance in the rearview mirror showed that he had disappeared inside of himself and that I wouldn't be getting a word out of him. It was just as well. At that moment I preferred the silence.

SOMETHING'S NOT RIGHT

A slightly altered version of this story was previously published in Jewish Noir (2015).

I could start this with when I first decided to kill Malcolm Pratt, but the problem in doing that is I'm not exactly sure when that was. The obvious moment would be when I first received his letter, but I don't think that was it. I'm not saying his letter didn't have me seeing red. It did. And yeah, I'll admit that if he had been in the same room with me when I read it I probably would've beaten him to death before I realized what I was doing. But even still, I think it was years later before I consciously made the decision to kill him. I might've at times fantasized about doing awful things to him if I had the chance, but those were really nothing more than harmless daydreams.

Even when I started sneaking away to a shooting range four towns over, I don't think I was seriously planning to kill him. Not even when I bought a 9mm pistol from a gangbanger in Bridgeport, Connecticut. I can't tell you why I did either of those, but I'm pretty sure the idea of hunting down and killing Pratt was still only a farfetched thought floating around in my subconscious, and not something I seriously planned on ever doing.

Maybe it was at the awards banquet last year. Pratt had sought me out to congratulate me for the success I'd been having, and when I looked into his round pink-scrubbed face, the lower half covered by his meticulously groomed facial hair, and saw the way he smiled at me in his innocuous, clueless way I realized he had forgotten about the letter he had sent me twelve years ago. Something about that bothered me far more than if he had remembered doing it. It was as if I was too insignificant for him to care about the torment he had caused me, and that he could just send me that letter and forget all about it as if it were nothing. I think it was then that the idea of killing him, actually killing him and not just fantasizing about it, took hold and became something real. But again, I can't be completely sure that was the exact moment.

Some of you reading this are probably familiar with my short stories and novels, and are naturally going to draw conjectures about me from them, and you'll think you have some clue about why I did what I did. You'll be wrong, but that's still your prerogative. Others of you who aren't previously familiar with my writing are probably going to assume I'm little more than a deranged psycho. I could be deluding myself, but I don't think that's the case.

I guess it's not too hard to figure out that I'm a writer given that this story is in one of my short story collections. Of course, the other stories before this one are fictional works, while this one is something very different. Let's for now call this a piece of creative nonfiction, although that's not what it is. Some of you might be thinking I've written a confession, but you'd be wrong. Badly. If you have enough patience to read on until the end, you'll understand what this really is and why I needed to write it.

Since it might help to explain why things happened the way they did, I should tell you that me ever ending up as a writer was a longshot, at best. It wasn't that I didn't read a lot as a kid, I did, sometimes a book a day, although they were mostly pulp fantasy or hard-boiled crime novels. Even with my interest in books, from early on I showed a strong aptitude in math, and later, computer science, and my future seemed pretty well mapped out for me to major in computer science in college and then get a job in the industry, which is what I did. But I've always had the writing bug lurking inside me, and at some point I started fooling around writing short stories. It started out mostly as a lark. During those early days I never thought I'd get published. I mean, I was a math and computer science guy with an engineering degree who was only able to fit three English courses into my college curriculum. How was I going to compete with the more literary minded English majors who lived and breathed this stuff and could quote esoteric writers I'd never heard of? I had no training, and really no confidence that I could ever write anything worthwhile. But then something happened. Something very unexpected. I found my voice and started writing stories that I believed could be published, and when I submitted them I had a small amount of success.

All of my early stories, and really my first six novels, fitted under the noir genre. These days publishers like to call every piece of watered down mystery and crime fiction *noir*, even when the story has a happy ending. They do this because they think noir is hip, and that if they slap the noir label on a novel it will help with its marketing. But there are no heroes or happy endings in noir. And there's certainly no hope. True noir is about the alienated, the hapless, the broken. Things start off bad in noir fiction and only get worse. Moral lines are crossed that can't be uncrossed and characters fight a losing battle to keep from tumbling into the abyss. The irony is that these very same publishers who are only too happy to hype any book with the slightest hint of darkness as *noir* wouldn't touch a true noir novel. And there's a good reason for that. Most readers want happy endings. They don't want to be bummed out by following a noir protagonist to his doom. And the last thing they want is to get into the head of a borderline psychotic narrator.

You might be thinking that whatever drew me to writing noir is relevant to what ended up happening, and I guess you could be right, at least somewhat. To be more clear about my situation, I wasn't just writing noir but a darker and more twisted version of it called *psycho noir*, which is where the protagonist's perceptions and rationalizations are just off-kilter enough to damn him to hell. Maybe that information could also be useful. I don't know. Without being too convoluted about it, let me explain what really attracted me to noir, which might also give some insight as to why I couldn't just forget about Pratt's letter.

When I first started getting my noir stories published, my cousin would always call up to make sure my wife was okay. Of course, he was only joking around, and I'd laugh it off with the big joke being that I must be as twisted and fucked up as my noir protagonists to be writing the stuff I was writing. And my wife would also always laugh it off when friends of hers would call up worried. She would explain to them that it was only fiction, and that I was a decent, gentle guy with a wild imagination, and I'd play along and pretend that that was all it was. The reality, though, was something different. I was able to write those noir characters as believably as I did because I identified with them. I understood them. As much as I'd like to pretend otherwise they were a part of me that I was able to keep well hidden. They were who I could become if I wasn't careful enough. I know that something about me isn't quite right, and that my cousin's jokes weren't as funny as he might've thought.

But enough of all that. It's about time I got back to Malcolm Pratt and the letter he wrote me.

As I mentioned earlier, I had some success right away with the short stories I was submitting, but my novels were a very different matter. I had a long, hard road with them where it took me nine years to get my first novel published. I would eventually see them all published, and once that happened they ended up getting a good amount of critical acclaim, but those early years were brutal. If I hadn't sold those short stories, I probably would've lost faith and quit entirely. As it was it was pretty dispiriting.

And now for how Malcolm Pratt fits into all this. After four years of my first novel collecting a thick stack of rejections, I read an interview with Pratt in a literary magazine where he raved about the noir author, Jim Thompson, who in the 50s and 60s wrote arguably the greatest psycho noir novels ever written. Pratt was a senior editor at the prestigious New York publishing house, Harleston Books, and I got excited as I read his interview and thought I found a kindred spirit. I wrote him a letter telling him that I shared his sentiments regarding Thompson's writing, and asked if he'd be willing to take a look at my first novel. He wrote back to tell me sure, send the book over. That he was always looking for a good noir read.

This is what I got back from Pratt less than two weeks after I mailed him my manuscript (and yes, I've recreated his letter from memory, which wasn't hard since every word in it was permanently burnt into my brain the same as if a branding iron was used):

After your earlier letter I was expecting at the least a diverting read, and not the excruciatingly hackneyed and clichéd disaster that you sent me. Your inane plot plodded along at a pace that made me want to drive sharpened spikes through my eyes, your characters barely qualified as cardboard cutouts, and your dialog was what I'd expect from a failing eighth grade creative writing student. The only thing that kept me reading your 'masterpiece' to the bitter end was my fascination over how shockingly bad it is.

I know you must be disappointed that I cannot offer even a single word of encouragement, but I can offer advice. Please, for the love of God, never put pen to paper again unless it is to compose a suicide note. Even that, I'm afraid, would end up as an unreadable mess.

Best of luck in your future career as a busboy or other such endeavor which I'm sure you'll be eminently qualified for.

Yours sincerely,
Malcolm Pratt

My wife knew within seconds that something was wrong. She must've read the letter over my shoulder (I must've been sitting down at the time, although I can't remember that part of it. I'm six feet tall while she's only five feet two, so it would've been impossible for her to read it over my shoulder if I was standing). At some point I became aware of her breath against my cheek, and then her calling Pratt a fucking asshole. I wasn't kidding before about seeing red. I was too enraged to talk, and couldn't have responded even if I had wanted to.

"You should rip up that letter," my wife said.

I think I shook my head, although I can't say for sure. My wife commented how it would be counterproductive for me to ever look at that letter again. "He's a miserable human being," she said. "He has to be. You can't let someone like him make you feel bad. That's what he wants. Please, dear, just forget about it and let me throw it away."

I somehow found my voice again and heard myself telling her that I needed to keep the letter for motivation. I still remember how odd and tinny my voice sounded, almost like it was echoing out of a cave, as I told her, "Every time I feel like quitting, I'll read that letter."

That left my wife stymied. Even though I'd been able to hide the part of me that I needed to hide from her, she still intuitively knew that my holding onto Pratt's letter was a mistake, but she really couldn't argue with what I'd said. After all, she had always been my biggest cheerleader, and if I was claiming that I could find motivation in that letter, how could she argue with that?"

"Promise me you won't dwell on it. Please?" she asked.

I promised her. And I knew better than to ever mention Pratt's letter to her again. Over the years whenever I felt bile rising in me because of that letter, I'd swallow back whatever rant about Pratt I was dying to unleash, and I'd leave the room so my wife wouldn't see my face muddled with rage. A few times she caught me, though. I'd be lost inside of my hatred toward Pratt, and I'd hear her asking me what was wrong, and it would surprise me when I'd look up and see her face pinched with worry. It would make me wonder how successfully I'd been hiding that other part of me. I would always tell her that I was only working out the plot of my latest novel or short story, and somehow she'd believe it. Or maybe she didn't. Maybe she only badly wanted to believe it.

When I think back on it, I must've made up my mind very early on to kill Pratt, even if I wasn't aware of doing so. That must've been what happened, because I never told any of my friends about that letter, nor did I ever mention Pratt to any of them. That had to be because I didn't want any of them connecting me to Pratt's death, although there never would've been any logical reason for them to make that leap. It's funny how the mind works, because I swear I wasn't consciously aware of making that decision back then, even though very early on I started plotting Pratt's murder.

Of course, I convinced myself that my plotting Pratt's murder was only a writing exercise, and that the information I was learning would be used in my later crime fiction. That doesn't explain the extraordinary caution I took. Since I was working as a software developer back then, I knew that while I could scrub clean any history of web searches from my computer that those searches could still be maintained at my service provider, and so I did all my searches on computers at libraries several towns away from mine. I learned a lot about Pratt's routine and his background and learned that he was from a wealthy, privileged family. He went to Yale, as was expected of him since four previous generations of Pratts went there before him, and since he had a trust fund he was able to join Harleston Books after graduation and not worry about the pittance that they paid him. What made my blood boil was when I read how he viewed it not only as his sacred duty to keep those that he decided were unworthy from being published but to do whatever he could to crush their spirits.

I soon found that it would be easy enough to kill him. Well, killing almost anyone is easy if you don't care about getting caught, but with Pratt I figured out how I could do it and get away with it.

Thanks to his grossly inflated sense of importance, Pratt had started what he called an Algonquin Roundtable for the twenty-first century where he cherry-picked other *great literary minds* so that they could meet once a month for lively discussions. It probably would've made me gag if I had to witness these blowhards in action, but it gave me a window of opportunity every month to kill Pratt. Instead of meeting at the Algonquin hotel, they met at a restaurant on a quiet street in the SoHo section of Manhattan, and their oh so lively discussions would breakup around two in the morning. While the other great literary minds would take cabs from the restaurant to wherever they lived, Pratt would walk to his apartment three blocks away. Once I started getting books published, I'd arrange for book events in New York so they'd coincide with these monthly meetings, and later those nights I'd find a quiet place to park along the route Pratt would use to walk home, and I'd wait for him. I could've killed him each of those nights except for two problems. First, I needed a car that couldn't be connected to me. As quiet as the street seemed at that hour, there was still a chance I could be caught by a hidden surveillance camera. And second, I had other things in mind for Pratt than a quick death on a Manhattan street.

The car issue turned out to be easily solved. Using a dark and secretive part of the Internet called the Deep Web, I found what amounted to a matchmaking site for owners who wanted their cars stolen for the insurance money and people like me who needed a car to either chop up for parts or to use for a crime. The owner leaves the keys in the car, and agrees to wait a day before reporting it stolen, while the thief agrees to make sure the car no longer exists after twenty-four hours. All this is arranged without leaving your real identity. The second issue of needing time to do what I wanted to do with Pratt resolved itself six days ago when my wife went to Florida to take care of her mom. At least I think it was six days ago. It's hard to keep track of time where I am now.

The timing of my wife's trip worked out perfectly as two days ago (assuming I've been able to keep track of the days correctly) was Pratt's last roundtable and I was able to arrange on the Deep Web to pick up a car in Hartford, Connecticut that same night. The bitter cold weather and the snow was perfect also for what I had in mind. I left my home in Boston at seven o'clock and by ten I had my car parked in a garage in Hartford. By eleven I was behind the wheel of a beat-up Ford Taurus sedan and heading to New York, and by one I parked on a SoHo street that was along the route Pratt took to walk back to his apartment. I settled in to wait for him.

As much as the cold and snow worked into my plans, there was a chance that Pratt had cancelled his roundtable because of the weather, and I felt a knotting in my stomach as I worried about that. Yeah, I know, logically it shouldn't have been that big a deal if he didn't show up since I'd always be able to try it again. But that wasn't quite true. I would need my wife to leave town again on a night that coincided with one of Pratt's roundtables, and that might not happen for years. And before that could happen again, he might disband his roundtable meetings for good, or he could end up dying on his own. As I sat in the car worrying about all this, I realized how much I needed to be the one to end his life—and not just end it, but make sure he knew why I was going to kill him. I couldn't possibly describe the sense of elation I felt when I looked in the rearview mirror and saw him trudging down the sidewalk, his head bowed to protect against the cold and snow.

Even with him wrapped up in an overcoat, and a big Russian-style fur hat covering his lowered head, I knew it was him. He never saw me as I snuck out of the car and crouched behind it. When I struck him on the back of the skull with the gun, I held back with the blow because I didn't want to crack his head open, but because of his furry hat all I did was stagger him. It didn't matter. He let out a soft *murrh* noise and took several drunken steps away from me before I caught up to him again. This time I knocked off his hat before hitting him a second time. Again, I hit him only about half as hard as I could've so I wouldn't kill him, and this time I mostly knocked him out. He was still making whimpering-type noises, but otherwise he wasn't moving as he lay face down on the snowy sidewalk. I used a plastic zip tie to bind his wrists together behind his back, and then flipped him over so I could make sure it was really Pratt. His eyes were half open and glazed and his mouth continued to move as he made his soft mewling noises, but otherwise he was out of it. I dragged him by his feet to the back of the car. He was a small man and it was surprisingly easy to lift him up and dump him into the car's trunk.

It took no more than thirty seconds from the time I first hit Pratt until I had the trunk closed on him. I gave a quick look around and the street was empty. Even if a surveillance camera had caught me in the act the police wouldn't be able to identify me. Even my wife wouldn't have been able to identify me with the getup I had on. Ski mask, bulky snow parka, ski pants, thick rubber snow boots. She'd never seen me wearing any of these items before. But even if I didn't have my face covered by the ski mask and my body draped under that massive parka, a surveillance picture wouldn't have done the police any good given the snow flurries and how dark it was.

I have to admit for the first ten minutes my heart was beating like crazy in my chest over worrying that someone might've looked out a window and called the police, but by the time I reached the Holland Tunnel I'd calmed down and was feeling only a grim satisfaction with how things had gone. I still had a long way to go before I'd be done with Pratt. A five and a half hour drive deep into the Adirondack Mountains and then several more hours of hiking, but the trickiest part of it was done. It was possible that Pratt could expire during the drive. Even if I hadn't knocked him mostly unconscious, he was sixty-eight and appeared frail, and he was going to be spending all that time bouncing around in the frigid trunk. If that were to happen it would be too bad, but it wasn't worth worrying about. At this point it was out of my hands.

The drive to upstate New York went by faster than I would've imagined, especially with how much the snow was picking up. It wasn't blizzard conditions, but it was still coming down at a good clip. It was funny how these large lapses of time seemed to pass by without me being aware of it. One minute I'd be driving through Poughkeepsie and the next it was as if I was just entering Albany, and it seemed to go on like that the whole trip, almost as if my mind was blanking out on me. Like I was numb and on automatic pilot. Whatever the reason it made it an easy drive, and fortunately I had enough presence of mind to pull over for gas when I needed it and to pay for it with cash instead of a credit card. I could not afford to have anyone trace me to where I was heading.

It was a little after seven thirty in the morning by the time I reached the spot that I had decided on months ago. The snow had picked up and had made the roads treacherous, but it hadn't slowed me down. I guess I must've been driving recklessly, as if I didn't care about anything anymore. It was an odd way for me to be feeling. I'd already suggested how much distress Pratt and his damn letter had caused me over the years, but I didn't mention all those nights where I'd wake up seething in my hatred for him, or how for months now I'd been obsessing about taking care of him this way. I couldn't understand the sense of regret I was feeling. Maybe it was because I had a premonition over what was going to be happening. I can't say for sure.

Pratt's skin had turned gray, kind of like a corpse's, but he was still alive, and was fully conscious. He must've been both cold and scared out of his mind with the way his teeth were chattering like one of those old novelty items. I pulled him out of the trunk and dumped him onto the side of the road, and then pulled him to his feet.

"Start walking," I ordered. As added incentive for him to head off into the woods, I shoved the barrel of my 9mm pistol against the back of his head.

He moved in a slow pace, which was probably all he could manage with his hands bound behind his back and the snow already halfway up to his knees with more of it coming down. With his Italian leather shoes and the tuxedo he wore under his overcoat, he certainly wasn't dressed for the hike in the woods that we were going to be taking. His shoes must've been ruined and soaked through within seconds of trudging through the snow, and he had to be absolutely miserable. Even though this is what I thought I wanted I found myself feeling a mix of regret and remorse. Before too long I started trying to think of some way out of killing him. We hadn't walked that far from the road yet, no more than half a mile. He didn't know who I was, and had no way of ever knowing, and it was doubtful he paid any attention to what type of car he'd been thrown into. If I left him where he was, he'd have a good chance of getting back to the road and having someone pick him up, and by the time that happened I'd be long gone. I had just about decided to do that when he came to a stop.

"I'm not taking another step," he stated, his voice surprisingly strong given what I'd put him through. "If you want to shoot me here, go right ahead, but I think you're too much of a coward to do that."

I couldn't back down then, not with him challenging me. In a way it would've been so easy to just shoot him and get it over with, but I wasn't ready to make that decision. Not with the buyer's remorse I was feeling.

"This was only supposed to be a kidnapping," I said. "There's a warm cabin two miles further into the woods where I was planning to stash you, but fuck it, I should be able to collect the ransom whether you're alive or dead."

I lifted the gun as if I was going to shoot him in the back of the head, and even though he was facing away from me, he must've sensed my action given the way he cringed. In any case, what I said must've made sense to him because he asked me not to shoot him, and he started walking again, albeit in a slow crippled pace.

Even though my heart was no longer in it, I couldn't give it up, at least not then. Maybe after we hiked another mile I could, but not then. We didn't go very far before he commented how my voice sounded familiar. "Do I know you?" he asked.

I have to admit I felt my chest seize up when he asked that. The idea of him being able to recognize me from my voice was ludicrous. We talked once a little under a year ago, although he was in attendance at the awards banquet when I gave my acceptance speech. Still, how could he possibly recognize my voice given the conditions? Not only did I have a ski mask covering most of my mouth, but with the snow and wind howling about it shouldn't have been possible. Logically, I knew he couldn't have known who I was. That at any time I could still turn around and I'd be safe leaving him alive. But even understanding that, when I barked at him to shut up, I made my voice lower and more gravelly than normal. That seemed to amuse him. A short time later he asked if I was from Boston.

"I told you to shut up!"

The damn question kept me from turning around. I had decided I no longer wanted to kill him. I could accept that the suffering I'd caused him over the last six and a half hours was a fair trade for all the rage his damn letter had inflicted on me. As long as I could be sure he hadn't recognized me, I could just walk away from this. The odds were good that he'd be able to make it back to the road and that someone would pick him up. Maybe he'd suffer some frostbite and hypothermia, but that would only enrich the story he'd be telling over and over again at his monthly roundtable. And if he didn't make it out of the woods, well, that would be an act of God, even if I didn't believe in any sort of God. All I needed to do was convince myself that he couldn't have recognized me, and I would've ended this without him dying. Or those others either. I had almost reached that point when he turned around to tell me he knew who I was. And then he told me my name.

"What is wrong with you?" he demanded. "I've been an advocate of yours. Chrissakes, I've been recommending your books to other editors I know. I told you this when I met you last year. So why in the world would you do this to me?"

My spine turned into ice when he mentioned my name. Now, though, as I stared at him it was as if my skin was burning up.

"You're a fucking liar," I said through clenched teeth. "An advocate, huh? What about the letter you sent me?"

"What are you talking about? I never sent you any letter!"

"Sure you did. When I sent you my first book."

"I don't know what you're talking about." He shook his head sadly at me. "I caught up with all your books last year ago, and I thought your first one was a solid debut."

I laughed at that, although it came out as something strangled deep in my throat. "Yeah? That's not what you wrote in your letter." I had his letter tucked away in my inside coat pocket, but I didn't bother taking it out as I recited it to him. As I'd already mentioned, I had every word of that damn letter forever burnt into my brain.

He gave me this odd look as he shook his head. "That must've been years ago," he said.

A red glaze covered my eyes. I could barely see past it. "Twelve years ago," I forced out, hating how my voice shook.

Even though his hair, eyebrows, and carefully cropped beard and mustache were encrusted with snow and ice, there was no mistaking the look of pity and contempt that he gave me. "I didn't read your book back then," he said. "That was a form letter I used to send out as my way of helping to separate the wheat from chaff, so to speak. The writers with true talent wouldn't let a letter like that discourage them and would find a way to persevere. But if that letter could help encourage the vast majority of wannabes who were bothering me to quit writing, then good riddance." He paused for a moment, his eyes turning every bit as icy as the weather. "I suggest strongly that you take me home now before you get yourself in even worse trouble."

He shouldn't have used that patronizing tone with me. He should've known full well by then that something wasn't quite right with me, and he should've been smart enough not to do that. If he hadn't used that tone, it was still possible that I would've let him live, even with him knowing who I was. But that tone ignited all the dormant rage inside me to once again boil up the same as when I first read that damn letter, and before I fully realized what I was doing I fired two bullets into his face. I think the first one hit him in the eye. I'm not sure where the second one hit him, but there was no doubt he was dead before he ever hit the ground. It was only after I fired those shots that I noticed the two hunters who were standing ten feet off to the side of me.

I had no idea how long they'd been standing there. I hadn't heard them approach, but I wouldn't have been able to in any case with the way the snow and the wind was blowing about. They were both only in their twenties, and they both wore these odd half frozen smiles, as if they thought they might've wandered over to where a movie was being shot, or maybe that this was only a bizarre practical joke for a TV show. The way I looked at them snapped them out of their stupors, and their goofy half grins quickly changed into something fearful and grim. Before they could raise their rifles, I fired two shots directly into the chest of the one on my right. When I turned my gun on the other one, my first shot missed wildly because of how he had dropped to the ground for cover. The split second I got off my second shot, I saw the end of his rifle barrel spitting fire at me, and then it was as if I'd been kicked in the stomach by an angry mule.

For a half hour, maybe longer, I laid on my back expecting to die. The snow was still falling at a heavy rate, and although my world had become a white haze, I saw things with a clarity of thought that I hadn't had for a long time, and I accepted that what happened had to happen. If I had been a different type of person I would've simply been pissed off by Pratt's letter and days later be able to laugh it off. But I wasn't that type of person. He shouldn't have indiscriminately sent out those letters. By doing so, eventually one of them would go to someone like me. What happened to him was inevitable.

At some point I realized I wasn't going to die, at least not then. Shortly after that I also realized that I could move. At first I just wanted to stay where I was and let the snow bury me. It hurt like hell and it would've been so easy to just let myself be buried under the snow and die out there. But I found that I couldn't just do that. Slowly, gingerly, I rolled onto my knees, and once I did this, I realized why the other hunter hadn't finished me off yet. My second shot had taken off the top of his head. Even though he was covered by a half inch of snow, there was still enough gore left behind from the shooting to make it obvious that was what had happened.

At first I was crawling on my hands and knees. I was trying to retrace my path and head back to the car, but the snow had covered up the tracks Pratt and I had made, and given my state of mind, I doubt I was going the right way. But still I kept crawling, and when I could I got to my feet and staggered along. I tried not to think about the bloody mess my stomach had been turned into, and I certainly tried not to catch even a glimpse of it. At some point I fell back to my knees and crawled along the ground as long as I could keep moving. And then everything went black.

When I woke up next the world had become painfully bright, like I was directly under a searchlight. I had the sense that there were people bent over me, but I couldn't really see them because of how bright it was. I didn't feel any pain in my stomach then, only a tugging sensation. Someone shouted, "He's come out of it! Put him under!", and as if a switch had been thrown everything went black again.

I found out later that a snowmobiler found me and called for a rescue crew, and while it was touch and go during the three hour surgery, the doctors ended up saving my life. By five o'clock the very same day that I shot Pratt and those other two men to death, I was lying on a hospital bed in the Intensive Care Unit, the middle of my body wrapped in thick bandages, my mind just barely alert enough to make sense of what the doctor was saying as he explained to me what had happened. While my mind was fuzzy and I was having trouble keeping my focus on what he was saying, one thing that struck me was how uncomfortable he appeared. I knew outside of him there was a nurse in the room, but there had to be someone else also. I could tell that from the way this doctor's gaze shifted to where this other person must've been standing. Even without that, I would've felt this other person's presence. After the doctor finished filling me in, he cleared his throat and told me the local sheriff wanted to ask me a few questions, and asked if I was up to it. I shook my head and closed my eyes, and let the morphine drift me back into unconsciousness.

It turned out that the sheriff was determined to speak to me that day. I know that because a nurse whom I later became friendly with told me that he had camped out in my room waiting for me to wake up from my morphine induced sleep, which didn't happen until after nine that same night.

He was a big rawboned man in his fifties with short cropped salt and pepper hair and a ruddy complexion. He introduced himself as Dale Grandy. As he stared at me, a hardness settled over his face and not a drop of sympathy showed in his expression for the near fatal injury I had suffered. He asked me if I remembered what happened. I nodded and told him in a voice that was barely a croak that I was shot in the stomach.

His eyes glazed when I said that. I knew right then that if he could've gotten away with it, he would poked a finger into my bullet wound until I told him everything he wanted to know. But he couldn't get away with it. All he could do with the doctors and nurses hanging around was ask me questions. I could lie right now and say I didn't understand the reason for his outward hostility toward me, but I understood it fully, which I'll explain later. What I didn't know at that time was whether those other bodies had been found yet. They hadn't been, which made sense since the snow would've covered any bloody trail I might've left back to them, but I didn't know that then.

"Do you know who shot you?"

I shook my head, and croaked out that I was guessing a hunter. "He must've thought I was a deer. I didn't see him."

"You're from Boston?"

I nodded.

"That's a long way from here. What are you doing in our neck of the woods? Did you come up here just so you could take a rifle shot to the belly?"

I think he was trying to make a joke with his last question, as if he were trying to establish a rapport with me, but there was no hiding his true feelings toward me. In any case I just told him it was a long story.

"I've got all night," he said, his lips twisted into a thin, harsh smile, another halfhearted attempt on his part to show we could be friends.

"I think it was last night when I was driving to New Haven? I don't know how long I've been out of it, but I think it was last night—"

"What day was it?" he asked, interrupting me.

I told him the day that I left to kill Pratt.

"It was last night," he said.

"Okay. I was driving to New Haven and like an idiot I stopped to help out what I thought was a stranded motorist outside of Hartford. It was a setup. I don't know whether he was out to kidnap me, steal my car, or do perverted things to me, or all of the above, but he forced me at gunpoint to get into the trunk of his car—"

"What type of car was this?"

I squeezed my eyes tight as if I was trying to remember it. Of course it wasn't too hard to figure out that the car had already been found. "Something old, beat-up and brown. I think it was a Ford Taurus?"

He nodded, letting me know I got the answer right.

"He must've driven all night with me in the trunk. When the car finally stopped, he pulled me out of the trunk and made me march into the woods. But he wasn't the one who shot me, because he was behind me, and I didn't see who it was in front of me. So it must've been a hunter."

My story was a doozy. That's what I do for a living. I make up stories, and in this case I did the best I could with what I had to work with. Just so you don't get the wrong idea, I didn't make it up on the fly right then and there. I started thinking about it when I woke up after the surgery. In any case it confused Grandy enough where I could see doubt enter his eyes. I wasn't sure what he had been thinking I had done since I was the one who was shot and I know now that the other bodies hadn't been found, but he still had had me pegged as someone who came to his town with bad intentions. Now he didn't know what to think. Before he could ask me anything else, I forced a couple of weak coughs that were even weaker than the voice I'd been using, and a doctor who must've been standing off in the background quickly stepped forward and ushered a reluctant Sheriff Grandy out of the room, insisting that I had answered enough questions for one night and anymore would be putting my health at risk. Grandy didn't like being chased out of there, but there was nothing he could do about it at that moment.

Once I was alone I thought about the story I had given and whether it could possibly hold up once those other bodies were found. I didn't know. There were several ways I could see of poking holes in it, and I was sure if I studied it more I'd think of others. One obvious way was that I had stopped at two gas stations during the drive up, and if either of the attendants that I paid cash to could identify me, then I'd be sunk. But how could they? I was wearing a ski mask at the time so there wouldn't be any photos from surveillance cameras, and at some point while I was staggering away from the murder site I'd lost the mask—I was feeling feverish, and vaguely remember ripping it off and tossing it. It wasn't going to be found. Not in that snow. So how could either of those attendants identify me? I knew once those other bodies were found, Grandy would know my story was a lie and that I was involved in those deaths, but could he prove it?

Whether it was the morphine, or because it fully exhausted me answering Grandy's questions and later worrying whether my story would save me, I drifted off again, and when I woke up the next morning, Grandy was waiting for me. The hostility he had shown me earlier was back, maybe double what it was before. He had to wait, though, before he could question me any further for the nurse to first take care of some things, and then for the doctor to examine me, and while this happened I prepared myself. He didn't bother with any niceties, and instead jumped right into it, asking me to describe the guy who kidnapped me.

"A white guy. Late twenties, thin, long hair. Bad teeth that were kind of brown," I said, as I gave him a description of how I imagined a typical meth user. "That's all I can remember. I really didn't get a great look at him."

"Tell me again why you stopped?"

"He looked like he needed help. I'd been having some good luck of late. I thought it would be a good karma kind of thing to do." I did a bit of acting then, making a pained face as if I were suffering from a toothache. "I didn't expect what happened next."

He didn't buy a word I was saying, but I wasn't going to let him know I knew that. Instead I shook my head angrily over what my imaginary kidnapper did to me.

"Why were you going to New Haven?" Grandy asked.

"Research. I'm a writer. I've been working out an idea for a new crime novel that takes place in New Haven. I headed out there somewhat for inspiration but mostly to work out some details that had me stumped."

He didn't like my answer at all. Again, if there weren't any doctors or nurses around he would've forced me to give him a different one. I could see it in his eyes. But since he couldn't do that, he asked me why I was dressed the way I was.

"Snow pants, snow boots, heavy parka, extreme weather gloves," he said with a harsh smile. "That's all stuff you'd be wearing to go hiking in the woods. I wouldn't think you'd be wearing that to New Haven."

"It was cold and snowing, and I expected to be outside a lot. That's why I dressed the way I did. I had a wool cap also, but lost it somewhere along the way."

"What about your car? You had your cars key with you. Why didn't your kidnapper take them?"

I shook my head. "I don't know. Maybe he was planning to take them later."

Grandy was frowning at my answer. A good-natured frown, though. An act. Like he thought he was about to catch me in a lie.

"What happened to your car?" he asked. "The kidnapper didn't have your keys, yet your car wasn't found anywhere along Interstate 84 like it should've been if you pulled over like you said you did."

I shrugged, while also thanking my lucky stars that I'd

left the parking garage ticket in my car instead of keeping it in my wallet. It was pathetic that this was his big gotcha. It gave me hope that I would get away with it. "It must've been a two-man operation," I said. "He must've had a partner tow my car. Maybe to a chop shop."

For a long moment Grandy simply glared at me. Then he took two photos from an envelope and showed them to me. These were the two hunters I killed, not that that was any surprise. If it wasn't for the morphine, I probably would've started sweating. But as it was I think I was able to maintain a placid expression.

"Neither of them kidnapped me," I said.

A muscle along the side of his jaw tightened. "They're locals. Did you see either of them?"

I shook my head. "You think one of them shot me?" I asked.

He didn't answer me. I don't think he was capable of answering me right then, and I knew why. He suspected those two boys were dead. The only thing that was keeping him from killing me at that moment was he wasn't sure. It was possible that I was shot in a hunting accident like it appeared, and that those two boys realizing it took off to hide and get drunk. Of course, that doesn't explain why he'd want to kill me even if he suspected me of doing what he thought I did. It's pretty simple, really. The first moment I saw Grandy, I could see the strong resemblance between him and one of those boys I killed. The boy could've been a nephew, but the odds were it was his son.

For the time being Sheriff Dale Grandy was done with me, and as he left I knew where he was heading. Back to the woods to search for his son.

Later around noon I was moved out of ICU to another part of the hospital. I guess they decided I was no longer in imminent danger. My new room had a TV set, and it was all over the local news about my being found in the woods shot in the stomach. Nothing yet about any other bodies being found.

UNLUCKY SEVEN

The new nurse assigned to me turned out to be a fan, and had read all my books. My doctor didn't want me doing anything but resting and recuperating, but I convinced my nurse to get me a pad of paper and a pen so that I could work on a final story that I owed my editor for what looked like would be my last collection. With her help I also got an envelope for mailing my story, and after giving her my email address and password, she was able to get the address I needed so I could mail this to my editor. I'd also arranged for her to mail it for me if I'm gone and she finds it in the nightstand drawer next to me. If that were to happen, as far as she's concerned I was discharged without her knowing about it and that I somehow forget to bring the envelope with me. That won't really be what happened. If I'm discharged or arrested, I'll make sure that this so-called *piece of creative nonfiction* that I've been working on like a devil possessed ever since Grandy's third visit will be destroyed and no one will ever see it. The only way this will ever show up in my collection is if Grandy takes me out of the hospital without anyone knowing about it. Or at least anyone being willing to admit they know about it.

Grandy's third visit was about an hour ago. He asked me about Malcolm Pratt. Of course he found the letter from Pratt that I had tucked away in my inside coat pocket. I told him how I had only met Pratt once and didn't really know him well. He didn't buy that, not with me having that letter. He told me that Pratt was missing in New York. He asked me if I knew where he was. I told him I didn't, and I could tell Grandy didn't believe me.

The reason he hasn't so far dragged me out of here and taken me to a quiet spot in the woods is that he still has a sliver of doubt because he hasn't found those bodies yet. But deep down he knows he's going to, and that's why he hasn't had my gloves or parka tested for gunpowder residue. He doesn't want to bring other law enforcement into this. He wants me to be able to disappear quietly after he finds his son.

Grandy's going to find all three of them. There's no doubt about it anymore. Not after the weather report I saw on the news minutes after his third visit. Following on the heels of this bitter cold and snow, they expect a warm front to be rolling in, bringing with it heavy rains. If they're right with their forecast, the snow covering the bodies will be gone by Monday. And I have little doubt that that forecast is going to be right.

Now you know why I needed to write this. So that sonofabitch Dale Grandy pays for what he's going to do to me.

ABOUT THE AUTHOR

Dave Zeltserman's books have been picked by NPR, the Washington Post, American Library Association, Booklist, and WBUR as best novels of the year, and his Julius Katz mystery stories has won a Shamus, Derringer and two Ellery Queen Readers Choice awards. His novel Small Crimes has been made into a Netflix film with the same title.

CPSIA information can be obtained
at www.ICGtesting.com
Printed in the USA
LVHW010935240921
698581LV00010B/400